Joe froze when he saw his daughter in the drug ringleader's grip.

"Don't hurt her. Do what you want with me, but let her go," Joe said.

"Touching, but she's easier to carry." Roman smiled. "Time to leave."

Aster struggled to get away, but Roman's hand clutched her neck, causing her to gasp for breath. He backed up with Aster between him and Linda's gun pointed in their direction. Linda aimed at the snowmobile to take it out and stop Roman's getaway, but Joe made a surprise rush attack to give Aster a chance to escape.

A flash of light blinded Linda and Joe for a moment, sending them staggering. Suddenly, the entire side of the nearby house was ablaze.

By the time they regained their bearings, Roman had Aster on the snowmobile. When the engine roared alive, Joe rushed toward them. Linda followed, but they were too late. The snowmobile sped off into the trees, snow billowing behind them...

Veronica Forand is the award-winning author of romantic thrillers, winning both the Bookseller's Best and the Golden Pen Award for the novels in her True Lies series.

When she's not writing, she's a search-and-rescue canine handler with her dog, Max.

A lover of education but a hater of tests, she attended Smith College and Boston College Law School. She studied in Paris and Geneva, worked in London and spent several glorious months in Ripon, England.

She currently divides her time living between Philadelphia, Vermont and Cape Cod.

Christmas Blizzard Rescue

VERONICA FORAND

LOVE INSPIRED
INSPIRATIONAL ROMANCE

LOVE INSPIRED®

INSPIRATIONAL ROMANCE

ISBN-13: 978-1-335-46846-8

Christmas Blizzard Rescue

Copyright © 2023 by Deborah Evans

For questions and comments about the quality of this book, please contact us at CustomerService@Harlequin.com.

Love Inspired
22 Adelaide St. West, 41st Floor
Toronto, Ontario M5H 4E3, Canada
www.LoveInspired.com

Printed in U.S.A.

For verily I say unto you, If ye have faith as a grain of mustard seed, ye shall say unto this mountain, Remove hence to yonder place; and it shall remove; and nothing shall be impossible unto you.
—*Matthew* 17:20

For Aster

Chapter One

The most wonderful time of the year was also the busiest and most stressful. Joe hustled around the inn, firing off orders to the cook, the head of housekeeping, and Claire at the front desk. Tiny details made the difference between a nice stay and a once-in-a-lifetime experience. "Don't forget that the Connors want a rollaway bed for their son in room 210. They also requested extra feather pillows."

Claire pointed to the computer screen. "Got it covered."

"And the Brakemans have a gluten allergy in their party. I think it's the grandmother, but you should have someone double-check."

Andy, the chef, nodded. "On top of it. I think we have everything under control, boss."

Joe caught his breath and looked at the hardest-working employees in Vermont. "I know you do. You guys are the best."

Evergreen wreaths tied with red bows and several tall Christmas trees decorated the lobby of the Red Pepper

Inn, welcoming the guests arriving for the holidays. The past year had been low on snow and lower on travel, but everything had picked up, and a decent amount of snow was expected by Christmas Eve, only two days away. The staff had prepared for this, and he trusted them, but it wasn't easy to give up control. Joe not only had his own savings tied up in the place, but he also carried the pressure of keeping thirty-three town residents employed in an area known for high unemployment.

Andy walked over to him after the staff withdrew from the lobby. "You okay? You're not acting like yourself."

"I just received a heads-up that the reviewer for *Yankee* magazine booked a room for tomorrow night. I want to be prepared." It was the first time the inn would be reviewed in a national publication. This could change everything.

"We're more than ready, and you've never been one to fall over when the pressure rose. Something else is eating you." With twenty-five years of history between them, Andy could read his mind. They'd been best friends since high school, even as Andy attended culinary school in Europe and honed his craft at five-star resorts in the Caribbean while Joe supported his mother and started a family at home.

"It's Aster. She's angry I missed her concert at school, and we're supposed to have our weekly pizza night, but I can't make it. There's a million details to perfect before the reviewer arrives."

"Send a to-do list to each department head. That's four people instead of one handling the details. And then go spend time with your daughter."

"She's not the easiest person to be with lately. The other night she blew up at me. She doesn't understand that the University of Colorado is too far and too expensive. She doesn't understand how difficult it would be for her to live so far away. And how can she turn down a scholarship to the University of Vermont? Instead of having a rational discussion, she lost it, so I grounded her. Now she's even angrier because she wanted to go to some party."

"Perhaps you're being a bit hard on her. She's top of her class, makes a killer white chocolate mocha at the Grounds Up Café, and on most days, adores you. So she blew up."

"She's never been like that before." That's what concerned him. They'd always agreed on most things and almost never argued. Now she wanted to move across the country, leaving him alone.

"Kids are allowed to get angry at their parents. I remember you raging about your father."

"I never would have yelled at my parents the way she did to me." Except that one time, when his father had gone a step too far and hit his mother, and Joe fought back. That was the day his father had left home for good. The memory burned.

"No one in town ever said a cross word to your father—he was too violent. You're not your father, and Aster does not live in fear of you. For that, we are all grateful."

Joe winced at the black-and-blue memories that woke him up at night. "Now you're making me feel horrible for grounding her."

"That's what friends are for. The reason the staff loves

you is your ability to listen to them." The staff loved Andy as well. Joe feared he'd leave again if the travel bug called to him. That loss would be hard to take. "Did you even try to hear her argument, or are you scared of letting her go?"

"Colorado is two thousand miles away. She's not ready for something so distant."

"I disagree. I think she's up to the challenge. It's you who isn't ready." Andy patted him on the back and waved goodbye.

Joe headed up to the suite he and Aster shared on the third floor. They'd been the dynamic duo, two against the world, ever since her mother, Ivy, had died when Aster was only two years old. More and more, however, they operated apart from each other. He hoped she'd remain close by, but she wanted to study molecular physics at the University of Colorado Boulder. Sure, the university had a good program—the best—but New England had a whole slew of amazing universities. The University of Vermont was only two hours away, and he could drive up to see her every few weeks.

He pushed open the door to their suite of rooms, then paused as he swallowed his urge to convince her of the benefits of being close to home. This wasn't the time. The gulf between them had grown too large, and he needed to compromise—something that would show how much he cared about her. Their relationship mattered, and maybe he could rebuild it with a pizza and the offer to lessen her punishment. "Aster. I'm back. I thought we could order a pizza and watch *It's a Wonderful Life*."

Silence responded.

"Aster?" he called out while opening the door to her bedroom. Her gray and white blankets were twisted off the sheets, cascading over the edge of her bed to the floor. Her laptop rested on her pillow, the screen black. A few pairs of jeans, sweatshirts, and a colorful array of socks and underwear covered most of the floor.

"Aster?" he called out louder, as though she would appear at the sound.

The quiet responded once more, sinking inside him and sending him rushing to the bathroom and into his own bedroom. She wasn't there. He'd told her not to go out. If she'd disobeyed him, he'd ground her for a year, take away her phone and lock her in her room.

He called her on her phone. No answer.

Texted her. No response.

He rushed downstairs to the lobby.

"Claire," he called over to the front desk. "Have you seen Aster?"

"No."

Tori paused next to him as she pulled a luggage cart filled with ski bags and suitcases toward the elevator. "I saw her about half an hour ago. She went out for a walk."

"Did she say where she was going?"

"No, she just walked out. I heard there's a party at Shiver Cabin tonight. Maybe she went there?" Shiver Cabin was on public land, and people rented it out, mostly in warmer weather. The place was close enough to town to be convenient and far enough to give people privacy. Too far to walk in this weather. He didn't want to show his annoyance in front of his staff, so he thanked Tori and went back upstairs to grab his coat and the keys to his car.

A few minutes later, he was searching the streets of Birch Glen in his Jeep. A smattering of snowflakes drifted through the air. The weather also gave him pause. Snow falling in the Green Mountains could turn an idyllic evening into a nightmare, especially when teenagers attempted to drive through it. Joe's search for Aster wasn't based on panic or anger. Instead, he was pushed on by a deep disappointment in Aster's decision and just a smidgen of something that didn't sit right, deep inside him.

A familiar petite woman walked alongside a large black Labrador retriever on the sidewalk ahead of him. Bundled up in a blue ski parka and white knit hat with shoulder-length hair peeking out, Linda Jameson carried herself with the confidence of a former marine. Back when they'd dated during their senior year of high school, he would never have imagined Linda becoming a soldier. A football running back with a string of scouts after him, he'd been mesmerized by how pretty Linda looked when she smiled at him. Had he looked closer, beyond her appearance and ever-present optimism, he would have seen a steel core and a mountain of ambition as well. Instead, he'd let her go.

He ignored the cloud of regret that hovered over him whenever he thought of her. He'd been the one to push her away. After she'd left for the marines, he ghosted her, too hurt by her ability to leave Birch Glen and the fate that tied him there. Then he'd married Ivy, and the world turned upside down for both of them. He lost Ivy, and

Linda lost her career. Her return to Birch Glen hadn't been the romantic reunion he'd dreamed of. There'd been nothing romantic about it.

Linda had come home eighteen years after graduation, when a helicopter crash ended her military career. Joe had wanted to rush to her parents' house and make sure she was okay, but he froze over what he'd say and how she'd receive it. She'd never reached out to him, either, only saying a curt "good morning" at the coffee shop in the same way she greeted all the other residents. Despite the chill between them, he went out of his way to grab coffee at the same time every morning with the hope of receiving two seconds of her attention. He'd been looking for an opening to say more but had nothing important enough to break the wall of indifference between them. Until tonight.

He slowed down his car and opened the passenger-side window and stared at the woman he should have chased across the world. Her dog remained patiently at her side, a dusting of snow coating his black fur.

"You haven't seen my daughter, Aster, walking around here? She's about five foot four with blond hair." He said it casually, as though he were more curious about his daughter's whereabouts than worried about her.

Linda's expression carried no hostility toward him; in fact, she appeared interested in hearing him out. "I know what Aster looks like. She's my favorite barista at the coffee shop. But no, I haven't seen her. A storm is headed here tonight. Did she have plans to meet anyone?"

Something in the way Linda stopped her walk and focused entirely on him encouraged him to share the full story. "Yes and no. There's a party at Shiver Cabin. That's why I'm worried. I told her she couldn't go, but I have a gut feeling she's headed there anyway."

She nodded. "Truth resides in your deepest intuition. I would trust it. Good luck. I can call you if I see her on my walk, if you give me your number."

"Thanks." Speaking to her for the first time in years about his disobedient daughter wasn't the smoothest way to reconnect with her, but Linda showed no judgment. He took the phone she offered and typed in his number.

As he drove away from her, he focused on his daughter. Something didn't feel right. He should take Linda's advice and trust where that feeling led him.

He drove up Sunset Gorge to the small dirt road that led to Shiver Cabin, an old log cabin maintained by the town. The road veered off into one of the more secluded areas of town. If there was a party, there would be parked cars or people milling about. When he arrived, he found nothing but a dark, abandoned cabin—not a car in sight.

Chapter Two

After Joe drove away, Linda continued walking block after block throughout Birch Glen with Zero, her five-year-old black Labrador retriever. She had so much to think about, especially with Joe's presence clouding her mind. Back in high school, she'd thought she loved him but knew she couldn't remain in town. She dreamed of adventures and world travel. After she'd left, Joe had to forgo college to care for his mother, who had suffered a stroke. He lost his scholarship and, over time, lost his mother as well. She'd tried to support him while enduring basic training, but he never responded to her texts, calls or emails. While the past was the past and she had long ago released the anger, some hurt still lingered in her heart.

She glanced at the snow swirling over the asphalt on the street. Joe had a rough night ahead of him if he didn't quickly find his daughter. She said a silent prayer asking for Aster to return soon. Although she didn't know his daughter well, she seemed like a decent kid.

Despite her own father's anticipated annoyance at her exercise, she stopped by the police station to visit him anyway. He wanted her to settle into a desk job, one where her dog would sleep under her desk for the day. Neither Linda nor Zero would be happy in that type of situation.

"Good afternoon, Vince," she said to the sixty-year-old receptionist, then paused at the sight of Joe. He appeared to have lived a thousand lives since she'd seen him only moments before.

He took no notice of her, fully focused on Officer Dylan Graham, a veteran on the force and a friend since kindergarten. "She's gone. You have to take a missing person report."

"She was seen walking out of the inn on her own. There's no evidence of foul play, Joe. She'll be back before sunrise," Dylan said, sipping on coffee and looking like he'd already had a long day.

"Is this how you run a police station? Leaving children to fend for themselves?" Joe's anger took Linda by surprise. He'd been intense and ambitious when younger but also thoughtful and controlled.

Dylan waved him away. "Joe, calm down. She'll be fine. If we sent a unit out to find every teenager who disobeyed their parents, we wouldn't have anyone left to deal with actual crime."

Joe's downcast eyes and the shifting of his feet side to side betrayed his fear. He was a terrified dad. A wave of concern washed over Linda. She fought the urge to place a hand on his shoulder to ease his stress.

"Did you go to Shiver Cabin?" she asked, stepping closer to him.

"No one's there." He swallowed what seemed like a whirlwind of thoughts and *what if*s.

"Joe Webster, I haven't seen you in here since someone wandered off with a television from one of the rooms at the inn last summer." Linda's father appeared behind them, dressed in a white buttoned shirt, navy tie and pants; his hair dusted with white, and his face creased from hours of smiling and sun. He acknowledged Zero as he greeted Joe but ignored Linda. Zero ran over to him and received scratches behind his ears. Her dog adored her father, and the feeling was mutual.

"Hey, Len," Joe said. "I'm glad you're here. I need help. My daughter's missing. You know she's not the type to run off, and with the snowfall this evening, it's not a great time to be out."

Dylan shrugged at his chief and stepped behind the reception desk to speak with Vince. From everyone's expression, Joe's problem wouldn't be receiving any extra attention tonight.

As though reading Linda's concern, her father placed his hand on Joe's shoulder and met his gaze. "I understand. I have three kids of my own—all grown adults—and I still worry about them. Truth is, there's been a car accident on Kingston Road. We have one officer directing traffic, a detective looking over the scene and another escorting the ambulance to the hospital. It looks like…" He cut short his sentence. "I don't have the resources right now to track down a missing teen who has only been gone an hour."

Joe sighed. "I don't want to take resources necessary for something more important, but…"

"She's the most important person to you. I get it," the chief responded, glancing over at Linda, his eyes softening. "Linda's safety keeps me up at night."

Linda shook her head. "Dad…" The transition from military police canine handler back to Chief Len's daughter had been rougher than she'd imagined. After years of working as an MP in narcotics detection and security at military bases on the West Coast, a helicopter malfunction turned her life upside down and backward. The accident had torn her ligaments, broken her collarbone and given her nerve damage in her left arm.

Zero had also lost his job after the accident by refusing to climb into a helicopter again. Linda couldn't blame him; she wasn't keen on flying again either. Not that she wanted to sit on a rocking chair on a front porch. There had to be some middle ground. So far, she'd found nothing that excited her as much as her old job.

"Once a father, always a father. You'd think there was a certain age when we stop worrying about our kids, but we never do." He stepped back to assess her. "I thought you were resting."

"I'm fine." She grimaced as she lifted her arm up and down showing a decent range of motion. Her father believed that a weak arm meant she needed more rest. He was wrong. Walking not only provided exercise but eased her mind as well. It wasn't easy going from a position of importance to someone with no importance at all. She had an appointment with a counselor who helped veterans transition to civilian life, and she'd sent out more than a dozen letters looking for a position where she could continue working with dogs.

"Joe, could you drive her home?" her father said.

Joe paused before answering. Perhaps he still wanted nothing to do with her, but something in those moody brown eyes pushed her to spend more time with him.

"Do you want some company while you look for Aster?" she asked.

Her question caught Joe off guard, but Linda's company was exactly what he needed. Not because it was a way to mend the rift he'd caused years ago—although they had spoken more in the past hour than they had in a decade—but because her presence eased his anxiety. Besides, he could use another set of eyes while he drove. Her life experience was an added bonus. "Sure."

They exited the police station together, her companionship loosening the tangle of thoughts he had aimed toward Aster. His daughter had never run away before, and she had a solid head on her shoulders. In many ways, she reminded Joe of Linda, a person with a big heart, a huge sense of responsibility and a call to adventure. So where the heck was she?

"Let me call the inn and see if she returned." If Aster was back home, maybe Linda could come by for some of the pizza Joe was craving.

She nodded and led Zero to a nearby bush to relieve himself as Joe contacted Claire at the front desk. Claire told him no one had seen Aster return, but she sent someone up to their suite just in case she had slipped by undetected. He held his breath, waiting for the flood of relief he'd feel when learning that Aster was home, but Claire didn't say that. According to the housekeeper she'd sent, the suite remained empty.

His argument with Aster earlier in the evening replayed in his mind. Every worst-case scenario popped into his thoughts. When he hung up with Claire, he shook his head at Linda's questioning look.

"No problem. She's bound to be close by. Do you have room in the Jeep for Zero?" She rubbed the huge dog's neck.

"He can have the whole back seat."

Zero must have sensed that Joe had made a decision, because he lunged forward and rubbed his head against Joe's leg.

"Sorry." She pulled him back. "When Zero isn't working, he's part cat."

"No worries. I love cats…and dogs." He petted Zero and bent down to look at the dog face-to-face. "What do you say, Zero? Want to come with me?"

Zero was still pressing into Joe's legs, tail wagging, tongue dangling from his mouth. He was a beautiful dog, with a wide chest, a broad square head and big amber eyes.

Linda clicked her tongue, and Zero turned away from Joe and sat at her side. They seemed fully aware of the other's thoughts and actions. Despite what the police chief had said, Linda appeared more bored than injured. She had a skill set that was far above searching for an absent teenager. From what he'd heard, she'd been formidable in the military police. A career she'd chosen over him. That wasn't quite a fair recollection of why she'd left; they'd both had huge plans at one point. She'd already enlisted, and he was set to play football at Ohio State, but his family imploded, and he remained in town to care for his mother. Instead of keeping in touch with her after she left, he'd tried to eliminate her from his thoughts, replacing her with Ivy, a beautiful woman who'd promised to never leave him. Three years after they had married and two years after Aster was born, Ivy had died in the car accident, leaving Aster without a mother and Joe without a wife. He'd never felt so alone in all his life.

Joe opened the back door of the Jeep, and Zero glanced up at Linda and waited for her to release him. She waved her hand toward the door, and he hopped inside and immediately lay down.

"I suppose that will work." Linda sat up front with Joe. "Where to?"

"I have no idea." He turned to her, his mood clouding over. Aster had only mentioned that one spot. If she wasn't there, she could be anywhere. "She's never done this before."

"Who's her best friend? Let's start there."

"She has a bunch of friends. I guess we could start with Natie and Payton." They danced at the same studio and acted in any play that had spots for all three of them. He hadn't pursued that avenue, for fear of embarrassing himself in front of their parents. In hindsight, her friends should have been the first people he'd gone to ask rather than harassing the police.

He pulled over into the parking lot for the post office and called Natie's father. "Hey, Nick."

They exchanged the shortest of pleasantries, and then he swallowed his pride and asked about his daughter. "I was wondering if Aster was over there."

Nick responded without hesitation. "Natie went out with Josh. They mentioned the movies. I told her to stay in town because of the snow. I don't trust Josh's old truck on these roads."

"Hopefully, it won't pick up until after everyone is safe at home," Joe replied.

"Do you want me to text Natie in case she runs into Aster?"

"That would be great. Thanks." After he hung up, he let out a long breath. Not that it helped. There were so many questions racing through his mind. Natie probably wouldn't reply to her father until after the movie finished, which meant Joe had to move on. That left Payton.

"Stay focused on the present, not the past," Linda said. "Even if the past is only moments ago. We've got this."

"You're like a walking fortune cookie."

She laughed. "When you deal in life-and-death situations, there's no time for a thesis-level analysis of every situation—but there are certain mindsets that can push you to better outcomes. You can beat yourself up over your decisions later when we're all sharing a hot chocolate by a Christmas tree. Right now, let's just think about Aster and where she went."

He nodded, trying hard to ignore that perfect image of Linda next to him by a Christmas tree.

Chapter Three

With Claire watching for Aster at the inn, Joe had no reason to return until he located her. Sure, he had the reviewer coming to town tomorrow, but nothing mattered over Aster's safety. "Let's stop by Payton's house, if you don't mind."

Linda's enthusiasm to help surprised him. He'd believed she'd written him off forever. She'd been legally obligated to fulfill her military contract, but he acted as though she'd run away from him. He deserved any hostility she cared to toss in his direction.

"To be honest, I'm going stir-crazy without a job to do. Zero is too. If my father had his way, I'd be at home on the couch with my arm in a sling. He's so overprotective, and it's driving me crazy."

"I get it. I do the same with Aster. She's so mad at me right now." And he'd pushed her right out the door. Not literally, but the result had been the same.

"You're her parent. I would think you need to put limits on her in some areas and trust her in others. It can't be an easy balance. You have a tough job, yet from what I've seen of her at the coffee shop, you've raised an amazing human being."

"Thanks, but recently…" Joe's words faded. He didn't want to voice all his insecurities.

He stole a glance at her. It felt both strange and comfortable to have her next to him. They'd dated for almost two years, and in that time, they'd shared their dreams for the future, their accomplishments in school, as well as the pain of his father's abandonment and the death of her grandparents. She'd become more beautiful, especially in the way she held herself, with a sophistication and strength that wasn't perceivable when she'd been a cheerleader. Her soft brown eyes, however, showed hints of sadness and loss as well. She was not the person who'd left this town years before. She had a maturity to her fashioned through time, travel and tumult.

He turned toward the outskirts of town, where hundred-year-old farmhouses and humble log cabins spread across the valley floor. Not an easy walk from the more populated town center but not impossible. As he drove by the high school, nostalgia attempted to ease his guilt and pain, but his heart might never heal after all he'd been through. The football field, empty of the crowds, slept under a scattering of snow. The mountains guarded it. A place of first kisses and icy breakups. The heavy emotions of those years crashed over him. His father had expected perfection from him, on the field and off, and when Joe was close to achieving a full scholarship, his father's absence forced Joe to abandon his future to care for his mother. Instead of asking for support in whatever way Linda could offer, he'd broken up with her, releasing her from the chains that held him back. She spread her wings and eventually flew all the way to California, and he started dating Ivy.

They remained silent for another mile—her searching side streets, him staring at the road. A sharp turn caused her to touch a hand to his arm to support herself. The warmth of old memories rushed over him, of holding her close and thriving in her energy. He steadied the car and hoped her hand remained.

"I was surprised to see you at the police station. I'm not saying it was a bit of an overreaction, but she's only been gone a few hours, and she was seen walking away from the inn," Linda said, her mannerisms more friend than interrogator, her hand still braced against him.

He shrugged. His only excuse had been panic, reliving the moment when his father had struck him and the police had seemed like his only option. "I thought lingering around the police station would give me access to information I couldn't learn on my own. Didn't work out so well. Your father never reveals even the slightest emotion, either positive or negative."

"My father is a wall of secrets. Even if something were happening, he always keeps investigations and bad news away from the reception area. Not to hurt you but to make sure the right resources have the best access to the situation. Now that I've been lead investigator on cases, I understand his discretion. I have no doubt if he finds something out, he'll contact you." She dropped her hand into her lap, and the warmth faded.

He pulled up to a small white house tucked between

maple trees and rows of hemlock. The home—at one time, a beauty—was thought to have been a Sears-kit house from the 1930s. Red and green lights covered various small bushes, and a large Santa on a train was inflated in the front yard. A few rooms were lit up inside as well.

"Do you want me to come with you?" Linda asked.

"I'm not sure. A marine could intimidate the family," he said with a smile.

"Oh, please. I'm the least intimidating person alive."

"I haven't seen you in action, but the military police are not shrinking violets."

She laughed. "No, I wouldn't call any marine a *shrinking violet*."

He opened his door. "Come on. You're far more of an asset out of the car than waiting in it."

The Dixon family had lived in Birch Glen only a few years, but the minute Payton arrived, she'd been friends with Aster. Joe had spoken to her mother, Trudy, several times at school events. They'd moved to town from Buffalo. A high school science teacher, Trudy was a great influence on Aster and her fascination with physics.

In an act of desperation, Joe said a prayer that Aster and Payton were sacked out, watching television and eating popcorn on the Dixons' couch. He'd love the opportunity to give her a mild scolding and take them all for hot chocolate. And best of all, his heart could rest after a strenuous evening.

Linda followed him up the stairs. She didn't know Trudy as well as most of the other residents, whom she'd known since she was in diapers.

When the front door opened, Trudy emerged, wearing a bright pink sweater over black dress pants and a teasing smile. "Joe? How are you?" Then she noticed Linda, and her smile fell into something less flirtatious and more polite. Linda understood. Handsome, a business owner and an overall decent guy—Joe was one of the most eligible bachelors in town.

"I'm looking for Aster. Is she here?" Joe asked.

Trudy shook her head. "She went out with Payton. I thought they went to the coffee shop."

Linda noticed Joe's posture relax at hearing that Aster was with Payton. If they located Aster quickly, maybe Joe would have time to grab some dinner with her—and Aster, of course, if she was interested. Linda's thoughts circled around how comfortable she was in Joe's company. Maybe they could resurrect a long-dead friendship, if not more.

"Do you know where they went?" Trudy said. "I was speaking to my sister when they left."

"I was hoping they were staying here."

Trudy looked out the window toward the driveway and frowned. She pulled out her phone and called someone. Probably Payton. "I did not give her permission to take my car."

After a few minutes of waiting for an answer, her posture grew stiff, and she turned toward the stairs. "George, get down here!"

"What?" A tall, athletic-looking teenager yelled back at her from the top of the landing. When he noticed the guests at the door, he repeated his question with a bit more restraint. "What's going on?"

Trudy waited until he walked down the stairs and then continued in a calmer voice. "Did Payton mention where she was going?"

"No, but there was supposed to be a party at Shiver Cabin. Maybe she went there."

"Why didn't you tell me?" Trudy asked.

"Why would I tell you about a party I didn't go to? I'm not one of your students who overshares every detail of their lives with you."

Trudy's demeanor wilted under his attack. "Did she say anything to you before she left?"

"No."

Linda bit back her disappointment. Until Joe had Aster in his sight, he'd be focused on her safety, as he should. Although she was with Payton, her whereabouts were still unknown, as Shiver Cabin had been deserted.

"I was up there less than an hour ago. It's empty," Joe said, staring at George as the kid shrugged at the news.

"I don't know, then," George said. "That's where everyone told me they were going. Parties change locations all the time. It's not like some big crime drama—it's a stinking party."

Linda had had these same arguments with her parents as a kid. She'd been questioned for every decision she made and fought back at her parents every chance she had. As an adult, she saw the whole picture: parents who'd wanted the best for their daughter, a daughter who'd wanted to be trusted and seen as an individual, and a lack of connection that would have bridged the misunderstandings.

He continued but focused his words at Joe. "Payton

never tells me anything. For all I know, she and Aster headed out to meet some of the guys from the debate team." He turned to Trudy. "Why don't you know where she is? You're her mother."

"Don't be so fresh." Trudy took a deep breath. "Do you know if they moved the party?"

George rolled his eyes, then grabbed his phone out of his back pocket. Everyone waited as he texted someone and paced back and forth, waiting for a reply. The ping sent his attention back to his screen. "Ian says it's now at the Primley place," he read off his phone.

"Thank you," Trudy said, the strain in her expression easing only after her son went back up the stairs and returned to his room.

Joe looked over at Linda. "It would be wise to drive up there and check on things."

"I would go, but Payton has my car." Trudy looked at her heavy wool coat hanging on a hook on the wall. "Three of George's tires went flat last night. That's what's making him so angry tonight. He hates being stuck inside."

"It's better if you stay here, in case they return before we get back," Joe said.

She nodded. "I've been so busy with exams and preparing for Christmas. I should know where my daughter is." Trudy rubbed her hand over her eyes.

"Don't be so hard on yourself. Christmas can be overwhelming." Linda understood that sentiment. Not only was this holiday filled with uncertainty for her, but it was also the one-year anniversary of the helicopter accident. The images of that night haunted her. She'd been

injured and unable to save her friends and colleagues.
Her only comfort was Zero. If she could hide out from
all the festivities, she would. Her parents expected her
to join them for Christmas service and dinner, but that
would be the extent of her seasonal observance. Her
heart wasn't into celebrating, not when she continued
to mourn the loss of so many people she cared about
and so much of her life too.

Trudy nodded but didn't appear ready to forgive herself. Single parenthood had to be an unforgiving job.
"She's driving a black RAV4. I should have asked more
about what she was doing, but I had cookies in the oven
and my sister on the phone. My priorities are upside
down. Please call me when you find out something. I
can't tell you how much I appreciate it."

Trudy's gratitude melted Linda's heart, despite the
woman's focus on Joe over Linda. It had been a long time
since she'd been useful to anyone. She let the feeling
warm her insides, giving her purpose and drive. Sure,
it was only one night, but it beat sitting on the couch,
feeling sorry for herself.

"We should start now," Joe said, noticing the snow
out the window. "The storm's picking up, and it could
be dangerous for everyone, even those who have four-
wheel drive if they remain there too late." Although Joe
should be able to navigate the roads, teenagers driving
cars, perhaps for the first time in such conditions, might
not manage it as well.

Shiver Cabin was only a mile or two out of town,
but the Primley place was more than five miles away,
down twisting dirt roads and at the end of a long, wind-

ing driveway up a mountain. They had to drive through the center of Birch Glen to get to the western side of the town.

In the Jeep, Linda thought back to something her father had told her. "A few weeks ago, Dad mentioned that Chuck and Fiona Primley rarely used the property, preferring to keep it for a week or two of skiing in January. So who would be hosting the party?"

She called her father. "Hey, Dad, I'm with Joe Webster. We're heading up to the Primley place to look for his daughter."

"Are you driving?"

She sighed. "Joe's driving."

"Okay." He sounded relieved, as though she hadn't scored the highest in her emergency-driving-and-vehicle-tactics training course. "Why the Primleys? They mentioned they were headed to Aspen for Christmas."

"Someone's having a party there."

"They have a college-aged son who knows a lot of the kids in town. He might be staying at the house for the holidays." Her father made knowing everyone's business a large part of his job, and more often than not, that information kept crime and misunderstandings down. "Be careful. The storm is supposed to intensify all night. Do you have adequate supplies?"

"We're not spending the night. If no one is there, we'll come right back to town." After she hung up, she stared out the window. Snow drifted across the road in a feathering of white.

The tension in the car eased slightly, despite the increasing snowfall. She lifted her shoulders to stretch them. Despite the incoming storm and the unknowns at the Primley place, excitement spun inside her, the kind she hadn't felt since before the helicopter crash. Her father had once described his love of law enforcement as not only a desire to help people but also an urge to run toward problems rather than running away from them. Linda had chosen the military police for the same reasons. Yet she'd spent the past year running away from her biggest problem: what to do with her future. Accompanying Joe seemed like a simple step toward returning to where she could do the most good. Besides, how difficult would it be to crash a high school party and bring home a teenage girl? Though it was a seemingly simple task, a million worst-case scenarios sped through her brain.

"Can we swing by my house first so I can grab my pack? If I learned anything from the marines, it was to take nothing for granted."

"This isn't a military operation."

"I hate to say it, but my father's right. There's a storm coming in, and I'd hate being stuck on the side of the road without certain gear." She shrugged. "I've never regretted being overprepared. And you have to pass by my street anyway."

"I have a first aid kit, a set of tire chains and a flare in the back."

"That's a start, but I need a better coat as well."

He turned down the road where her parents had lived for the past forty years. When they arrived at the house, Linda ran inside.

Her mother was standing there, concern worn like a silk scarf. "Where are you going? There's a storm coming."

"I worked for eighteen months in the Afghan mountains with minimal infrastructure. I'll be fine." A recitation of Linda's service accomplishments had become the standard response to her parents' words of caution. They had no idea what level of hell she'd existed in. Yet they worried about her driving around a Vermont village.

She ran upstairs and grabbed her pack. Zero's training harness was draped over the small desk chair. She grabbed that, too, just in case. When she arrived at the bottom of the stairs, her mother held out two coffee mugs.

"Two?"

"Your father saw you leaving with Joe Webster. Joe likes his coffee black."

Linda lifted a brow. "How would you know that?"

"He's a regular at the Grounds Up Café and so am I."

"When there's one coffee shop in town, I suppose it's inevitable." Linda took the mugs and waved goodbye to her mother. She didn't have time to interrogate her about Joe and what she knew of him in the past few years—something she should have bothered doing when she'd arrived in town, not now when she was driving around with him.

While she was inside, Joe had put the chains on the tires. He stood up and wiped his hands on his thighs when she arrived. She handed him one of the mugs.

"You had time to make coffee?" He took a sip and moaned in appreciation.

"My mother lives off of coffee. She's makes a large pot in the morning and pours it into a Thermos to stay hot. She insisted we have something warm for the ride. She'll never stop caring for me."

"That's the best kind of mother." The absence of both his mother and his wife must have felt like an Atlantic Ocean–sized hole in his life.

"You can borrow my mother. I think she'd welcome someone else to worry about and spoil rotten." Her mother had always been supermom and the best teacher at the high school. Super involved with the students, the girls' soccer coach, and one of those people whom teenagers could rely on when life became hard. She'd been voted Teacher of the Year over five times.

"I may take you up on that. Liz Jameson seems part mother, part teacher and part warrior." And from the wistful look on his face, he wasn't lying. He'd been alone for so long, handling the inn, his daughter and the ghost of his wife. As annoying as her mother was, her love for Linda and everyone around her never was in doubt.

She put her pack on the floor and secured Zero in the back seat with his harness attached to a seat belt. When inside the house, she'd also grabbed better gloves, a neck gaiter and a dark blue shell to wear over her ski parka.

"Ready to go, or are you loading up some snowshoes and a box of doughnuts as well?" Joe asked, looking up from his cell phone with a slight grin.

"Doughnuts would be wonderful, but I'm ready to go

as I am." She glanced out at the gusts of snow and prayed for a break in the weather. Otherwise, it was going to be a cold and dangerous night.

Chapter Four

The wind pushed into the side of Joe's Jeep. He gripped the wheel to keep the vehicle moving straight as he drove out of town and onto Route 100. He'd have to follow it a few miles to a turnoff for a hidden dirt road that would guide them through the Green Mountain National Park to the Primley place. On a clear day, clusters of white birch trees and sugar maples covered the valley floor as the river meandered alongside the drive like a good friend. The snow, however, covered that view with increasing flurries of white, reminding him of the dangerous conditions that were to come overnight.

"Are you okay?" Linda asked.

"Of course," he said, but he wasn't. How could he be? His daughter was so far out of town and away from the safety of Birch Glen. Dread, an old friend of a feeling, traveled beside him down the wintry road, in the same conditions that had killed his wife. The emotion had stood with him when he buried Ivy in the small graveyard next to the mountain chapel and remained on his shoulder as he parented his only child. Now it was amplified.

Snow covered the dirt road up the mountain. Faint tire tracks offered Joe some hope that he'd find Aster there. As they turned a corner, the Jeep hit a patch of ice hidden under the fresh snow. The chains held and Joe managed to keep the wheel steady, but the idea of what could have been if he hadn't taken the time to secure them set his nerves on fire.

"Do these kids have a death wish, coming out here in this weather?" he shouted.

Linda reached out to hold the dashboard, but otherwise her expression remained neutral. "Just keep moving. The last thing we need is to lose momentum up this hill and stall on the side of the road, especially with the possibility that drivers far less skilled than you might be coming toward us."

That thought hit him hard. The roadways were dangerous and would become perilous, yet Linda sat next to him, calm and assessing the situation with professionalism. The conditions became more hazardous as they climbed in elevation. The last time a storm had hit so quickly, he'd been busy at the hotel when Ivy rushed to the store for the ingredients to chicken parmesan—Joe's favorite—leaving Aster with Claire at the front desk. As the grief crept over him, he gripped the wheel tighter. Ivy had died on a patch of ice because she loved him. Joe had never forgiven himself. Now Linda was sitting next to him as he struggled up a mountain pass.

After fifteen strenuous minutes, they arrived at a large clearing with a monstrous McMansion ski chalet.

The Primleys had bought the land in the early 2000s and created a rustic Alpine castle that had enough open space inside the house to use up half the available energy in the region. Gossip in town said that the house had thirteen bedrooms and a marble floor in the foyer. Although they'd poured money into the building, they refused to make the driveway accessible in anything but warm and dry weather. A better investment would have been for a more modest home with a switchback-paved road, but people rarely invested in the right things.

Five cars sat parked by the house, one of them Trudy Dixon's black RAV4. It had less snow on the roof than the other cars but enough to tell him they'd been there longer than a few minutes. The lights were on in the house, and as Joe opened the car door, loud music echoed across the yard.

He headed to the front door, with Linda following. He knocked, but no one answered. He wasn't surprised. Who could hear with all that music blasting?

"No answer?" she asked.

"The door is locked. Let me try to see through the window."

He peered into a large picture window. Several kids were seated on overstuffed furniture, eating pizza and laughing. He banged on the window and waved his arms, feeling fairly ridiculous at this point, but he wanted his daughter back and didn't care what her friends thought of his parenting techniques. When he'd become a parent, any thought of being cool went out the window. He'd rather protect his daughter than earn points with the town's teenagers.

One of the boys saw him after what felt like ten minutes of waving his arms. He headed to the front door. As it opened, the boy stared at him. "Hey, Mr. W, what's up?"

"I'm looking for Aster. Have you seen her?"

"Sure. She arrived about an hour ago."

An hour ago? While he was scrambling around town looking for her, Aster had been enjoying herself at a party. The snow conditions should have been a warning to her to not travel far from town. He couldn't handle losing another loved one to the elements. "Do you know where she is right now?"

"Everyone scattered. Some went upstairs, some went for a snowmobile ride. The usual."

"Can we come in?" Linda asked.

"I mean, it's not my place, but Noah was pretty open about letting anyone inside, so I doubt he'd have a problem with it."

"Noah?" Joe asked.

"Noah Primley. His parents own the house. He invited the whole senior class and a few of the juniors too. He disappeared with some guys just before Aster arrived."

Joe glanced around, looking for Aster. "Do you know where they went?"

"Like I said, everyone scattered." The kid nodded his head as though that explained where half the party had gone.

Linda walked past both of them and into the living room and greeted a few of the kids. Joe followed. He scanned the room for Aster or Payton but didn't see either of them among the seven or eight high school students he recognized from around town. Natie, who was supposed to be at the movies, sat entwined with her boyfriend, Josh, on the couch. Dressed in a University of Vermont sweatshirt, she nibbled on a slice of cheese pizza, oblivious to anything going on around her.

He headed to her first. When she noticed him, she sat up and put her pizza on a paper plate. Josh slid a few inches away from her and remained silent.

"Mr. Webster, what are you doing here?" she shouted over the music.

"Looking for Aster."

"She's not in trouble, is she?"

"I just need to speak with her." The snow coming down would not let up for hours, and this was not the easiest place to leave.

Then he saw the beer in Johnny Gordan's hand, and his stress racheted up several notches. If anyone tried to drive home in blizzard conditions with beer zipping through their bloodstream, they could lose control and hit a tree—or worse, end up a white cross on the side of the road.

His composure slipped, and he nearly knocked the drink from Johnny's hand. "Where is she?" he asked through clenched teeth.

"What's going on?" Linda arrived next to him.

"Just hanging out." Natie ignored Joe and turned to Linda, who gave off a much calmer demeanor.

"Your father said you went to the movies," Joe said.

That comment changed her expression. "I… Ah…"

Josh leaned forward. "The movie theater had a malfunction, so we thought we'd come here. No biggie. Noah supplied all the food and drinks."

"Where are Aster and Payton?"

Natie shrugged. "I think they went snowmobiling. I heard a few engines head off."

"In this weather?"

"It wasn't so bad an hour ago."

"There could be over two feet of snow tonight."

This news did not create even the slightest stir in the crowd. The music continued, and the party recommenced, leaving Joe and Linda standing awkwardly in the room—except Linda didn't seem out of place at all. Her casual movements kept the kids at ease, yet if someone were to concentrate on her behavior, they'd notice she was on high alert. Joe had. Her eyes darted from corner to corner, and her attention was intent and focused.

Aster's absence pressed on Joe. Until he saw her, he couldn't relax. "I'm going to check upstairs."

"I'm coming with you," Linda said. "Someone needs to have your back."

"Funny." Although she was probably serious. After all the training she'd received in the military, she was more an asset in these situations than he was.

At the top of the stairs, they moved from room to room. One of the doors was locked. The amount of horrible thoughts and images that ran through Joe's head nearly crippled him, but Linda stepped forward and pounded on the door. "Open up." The authority coming from her voice had the person inside calling out to her within seconds.

"Just a minute."

"Now."

The door opened, and Linda stepped in front of Joe, probably to protect whoever was behind it from a father's fury. She didn't have to worry; his anger never came out in physical violence, although he had been known to raise his voice to unacceptable levels when he'd first been married. A few years of counseling had taught him better ways to express his frustration.

The scene was exactly what he'd expected: a young couple in bed. At least their clothes were on. Neither Aster nor Payton were in the room. The unknown girl didn't say anything as she fled to the attached bathroom, her face crimson.

"Have you seen Payton or Aster?" Linda said to the remaining boy.

He stared up at her as though assessing the danger level.

"Payton's car is here. Where are they?" Joe said, his diplomacy fading.

"They arrived a while ago. I haven't seen them since I came upstairs."

Linda and Joe continued their search down the hallway, not finding anyone else. In the last room, they pushed open the door and found a mess. Not a teenager's cluttered bedroom—more a ransacked room. Pictures were smashed on the floor, drawers had been pulled out and a red spot stained the carpet. Blood?

He cleared his throat. "Something's wrong."

Linda nodded. "I agree."

Chapter Five

Joe ran downstairs. Linda followed, her focus turned away from Aster's whereabouts and toward the cause of the blood—or whatever it was that looked suspiciously like blood. She scanned the stairway but saw no additional red drops. She turned around and went back up the stairs, back to the room. There was a stairway at the end of the hallway, down to the kitchen, and sure enough, another red droplet was on the wood of the top stair. She stepped carefully next to it and found another one two steps below. Joe came up behind her.

"What are you doing?"

"Trying to find if there is a person bleeding." She pointed to the drops and continued down the stairs and into a mudroom just off the kitchen. "It could be a cut from the broken glass upstairs. Maybe they stepped on a shard of glass—" She paused. There was blood on the handle of the door going outside. Joe nearly pushed past her, but she gripped his arm. "I don't know what we're going to encounter, but we need to continue cautiously.

Someone had enough anger issues to destroy the bedroom in such a manner. I prefer having the upper hand when I walk up to a person like that."

Joe nodded and followed her outside. A motion light turned on. It illuminated a nightmare. On the ground was a boy, no older than twenty, dusted over with snow and lying in a pool of blood. He'd been shot in the chest.

Linda rushed to the boy's side and examined him. She looked over at Joe and shook her head. "Call 911."

Joe glanced at his phone; it wasn't in service. He froze, looking back and forth between the boy and the house. Aster's safety had to be influencing his actions.

"Go inside and find one," she said, needing him to do something instead of panic.

When he returned, his hands were clenched tight. "The phone inside has no dial tone."

"I saw a satellite dish out front. I bet they use satellite internet to make calls. These heavy storm clouds could limit access." She searched the area for anything that would help them determine what had happened, while trying to protect any evidence left behind.

"Aster should be here. Where is she?" Joe shifted from foot to foot and stared out into the darkness.

"We can't do anything for this boy, but we can help the others." She stood up as the back door opened.

Natie appeared in the light of the doorframe, staring beyond Linda and Joe to the blood-stained crime scene. Her piercing scream brought two others outside.

Linda rushed toward her, trying to settle her down. "Do you know who that is?"

"It's Noah." She paused, her eyes displaying a mountain of pain.

"Noah Primley?"

"Yes."

"Did you hear a gunshot?" she asked.

Natie wrapped her arms around her chest. "No, but the music was so loud—and then the snowmobiles revved up and drove away."

Linda turned to the others. "Did any of you hear anything?"

They shook their heads. She escorted them back into the family room, away from the gruesome sight, and told everyone to stay away from the body. She then shut the music off. The silence echoed off the walls, removing all comfort from the large, rustic family room.

"Does anyone have a phone that has service?" She hoped one carrier was helpful enough to allow service in this desolate area of the state.

There was a collective "no" in response. They needed to get help, and they needed to find Aster and Payton.

"Where's Aster?" Joe asked, as though he hadn't asked the same question only minutes before.

"Maybe Payton and Aster went outside with Noah's friends," a boy in a Bruins shirt called out from the bar.

"Who? Did you recognize them?" Joe said, tossing out rapid-fire questions. "Where are they?"

"The guys went to Noah's bedroom," the boy said. "Payton and Aster went into the kitchen for cups or something. None of them came back, but we heard the snowmobiles driving off. I just thought they went for a ride."

Linda returned to Natie. "Is that what happened?"

She had paled and seemed about to be sick. Linda went to her and placed an arm over her shoulder. "Are you okay?"

She nodded. Linda led her to a place to sit down and tried learning anything else she could about Aster's whereabouts and who had last seen Noah alive.

Natie finally caught her breath. With tears in her eyes, she said she was sorry.

Joe started outside to look for them, but Linda remained behind in the family room. He turned to see what she was doing. Someone was dead, and his daughter was missing. The whole situation was a mess. He nearly called out to Linda but held back.

Linda had crouched in front of Natie and placed a hand on her shoulder. "Why are you sorry?"

"Josh started drinking as soon as we arrived here, and I didn't want to drive home in the car with him. I didn't know what to do because no one else was leaving until tomorrow. Someone told me to text Payton for a ride home. She's always game for bailing me out when I do something stupid, so it made sense. After I texted her, Josh became so sweet and apologetic, and Noah said we could spend the night. It seemed like the perfect excuse to delay leaving. When Payton and Aster arrived, I told them I wanted to stay. Payton was furious I'd made them come up here for nothing. If I'd known what would have happened, I never would have gotten her involved."

Linda nodded. "It's not your fault. Reaching out for a ride under those circumstances is always the right choice.

Right now, though, we're trying to understand what's going on."

Josh sat on the other end of the couch, his focus seeming blurred by the alcohol.

Joe stepped back into the center of the room. "Have any of you seen the men who went up to Noah's bedroom before?"

"Jeff, the younger guy, comes to town sometimes," one of the boys called out. "I've seen him at the Grounds Up Café."

"With who?"

He looked out the window and shrugged. "I don't remember."

Linda stared at one of the four guys in the room, his immense size more indicative of a center forward for a football team than a cowering teenager. "Has anyone else seen Jeff in town?"

They all shook their heads, not one set of eyes facing her. Perhaps they'd hand over information at the police station.

Linda squatted beside Natie. "Are you okay?"

She sniffled and leaned into her boyfriend. "I don't know."

"It'll be okay. One step at a time." Linda turned to Joe. "There's far too much going on here—a gunman or two on the loose and missing persons. It's now a crime scene, and I know we should keep everyone in place, but the thought of anyone else being shot because we asked them to all stay put doesn't sit well with me."

"What are you going to do?"

"Send them home before the blizzard shuts everything down, then get help."

She walked in front of the fireplace and faced everyone. When she pulled out her phone and took a few photos of every kid in the room, some of them scowled at her intrusion. Joe stepped up next to her to add some moral and physical support. Her actions made sense. The pictures provided them with information for law enforcement but would still permit the kids to get to safety.

"Okay, can I have your attention?" She spoke with the authority drilled into her in the marines. Everyone stopped whispering and stared at her. "I wouldn't normally recommend this, but under these circumstances, I think you should head back to town. The snow is only going to get worse, and I need one of you to contact Chief Jameson at the police station. Tell him everything you know and send assistance up here.

"Who hasn't been drinking?" She gave them a look as frightening as a high school vice principal on senior-prank day.

Five students raised their hands. She drilled them about their ability to drive in slippery conditions and asked if they had four-wheel drive or all-wheel drive and decent tires. Two of the sober kids didn't want to drive in this weather. Linda looked over the three remaining; they seemed not only sober but levelheaded. They introduced themselves as Jailah, Marjory and Camilla.

"Okay, if you feel capable of handling this weather, you three are taking everyone back to town. Be careful going down the mountain. Allow enough room between each car. Make sure all the cars get down the hill before you head to town. No car left behind." She waved them all to gather their things and pushed them outside. "Head straight to the police station to give a statement. If you don't, I will be following up, and your name and photo will be handed over to them when I get back to Birch Glen. Call your parents from there. You can retrieve the other cars tomorrow or the next day." She jotted down the names of everyone in the room.

"What are you doing?" Joe said, following her outside. The ghost of Noah followed him out the door, haunting his thoughts and reminding him that his beloved daughter was somewhere up here, in danger. Aster had to be their focus, not arranging a carpool back to town for the kids who were safe.

"I don't want anyone else hurt. If someone comes back with a gun, it will be over thirty minutes before help will arrive." Linda's seriousness shook him back into a more rational state.

She waved to Camilla as she drove away. Valerie and the mayor's daughter, Aska, were passengers. They all waved in reply, but not one of them was smiling. The significance of what had occurred subdued even the most confident of them. Without any hesitation, Linda had taken control and sent them safely back to town. While they were safe and leaving, no one knew where Aster had gone.

Joe went back inside while Linda played parking attendant. He searched the whole house, then looked inside Payton's unlocked vehicle.

As the last car left, he saw Linda take Zero out of

the Jeep, throw on her backpack and return to the front door. He'd forgotten about Zero while they were dealing with all the chaos inside.

"Why didn't you bring your dog inside when we arrived?" Joe asked, scanning the lawn and garden.

"To be honest, I thought we were going to break up a high school party. He wasn't trained to herd teenagers. If one of them panicked, someone could get hurt. Safety for him, safety for them. Noah's death and Payton and Aster's disappearance changes everything. If we can locate footprints headed away from the house, he could track them even under a light layer of snow. Too much snow, and it will be more difficult to follow the scent."

"I'm pretty good at tracking deer in the snow." He hoped he could use his own skills to help find his daughter.

"Good. Between his nose and our experience, we have a chance at locating her if she went on foot."

Chapter Six

Linda looked around for any footsteps leading away from the parked cars toward the forest. She didn't see any, so she returned to the back of the house. The blood had frozen, and a thin layer of snow preserved Noah's death. She said a prayer for him, more to ease the ache within herself than to tell God about Noah's presence. His life had already ascended; only his body remained. She'd seen death a lot as part of the military police. It never got easier, no matter who had died.

Zero had been trained not to disturb crime scenes, but he pulled closer to smell the area. Linda let him for a moment, then pulled him back. "Okay, Zero, leave it."

Zero understood and looked up at her for his next command. All she wanted was him to walk beside her without pulling on the slippery surface. If they found tracks, he'd have plenty to do.

She hoped the high school students would do as she'd told them, because her father would have a police unit driving up here within an hour. They could handle the

investigation and forensics. She and Joe needed to focus
on finding Aster and Payton.

Two sets of footprints left the area near Noah's body
toward a covered carport, where newly made snowmobile tracks headed into the forest. Two snowmobiles.
The footprints leading to the carport were too large to
be Aster's or Payton's. That was good because there was
no way she and Joe could follow a snowmobile on foot.

As she headed back to the house, she noticed a faint
set of footprints with more snow covering them than the
ones leading to the snowmobiles. She looked closer and
saw another set a few meters away—smaller shoe sizes
that headed to the tree line but stopped. They must have
been standing under the boughs of some pine trees for a
while, maybe having a conversation, maybe staying out
of the snow. She followed them farther. If they'd been in
that location when Noah was shot, they might have seen
the murder. If Linda were a frightened teenager in such
a situation, she'd head farther into the woods to hide.
She refused to tell Joe her assumptions. He had enough
concern over her safety that she didn't need him to be
worried that Aster was a witness to a murder.

Zero nudged her. He could be cold or bored. She rubbed
his head. He should be able to follow a trail left by Aster.

"Do you have anything of your daughter's I can use
as a scent source? A hat or shoe of hers would hold the
most scent. Something she wore recently?"

Joe went back to the car. "I have her Red Sox cap.
She wears it all the time."

"Perfect. Leave it there so you don't add your scent
to it. We want Zero focused on one person. And maybe

we'll locate Payton as well." Hopefully, before the two men could find them. Time was of the essence in weather like this, but rushing into an unknown situation without proper preparation made no sense. The wilderness could kill them as easily as the gun the men carried. They had to have sufficient resources if they traveled farther than the manicured property around the house.

She grabbed a stick off the ground and used it to lift the hat out of the back of the Jeep. She placed it into a freezer bag she had in her pack, to keep the scent as isolated as possible. Then she attached a long lead onto the back clip of Zero's harness and switched out her gloves for a heavy leather pair to protect her hands when Zero pulled. He'd been known to pull her off her feet when excited by a scent. In this weather, she didn't have as much of a grip. Instead, she needed to rely on her training and understanding of Zero's movement and reactions. After a lot of training, she'd learned to be aware of his body language when he followed a track. That knowledge kept her in balance with how much he would be pulling, preventing most accidents as they tracked their target.

They went back to the door Payton and Aster had left out of nearly an hour before. Linda showed the dog the hat, opening the freezer bag and letting him sniff it. "Can you locate Aster for us, Zero? Seek."

When Zero's body language indicated he'd caught the scent on the ground, Linda sealed the hat in the bag and put it in a side pocket on her pack.

Zero led her toward the pines away from the house in the same direction as Aster's footsteps. He proceeded under the trees to a small trail opening about a hundred meters from the house. She let him have more leash. His nose went to the ground, and he headed into the forest. The two sets of faint footsteps under the snow were still visible. The trail had trees bunched together that prevented the snowmobiles from following directly.

Joe pushed ahead of them, nearly racing down the trail. She could understand his stress. This was his daughter in the woods. She couldn't imagine the strain he was under, but she knew her own job and would perform it best if he listened to her.

"Joe, you need to let Zero lead," Linda called out to him, stalling his run. "He has the scent, and the less we disturb the trail, the faster he'll be able to guide us to Aster's location. You search for any sign of them, and I'll focus on the dog. Listen, too, for anything unusual."

The snow provided a brighter path to follow, but the storm clouds and arrival of nightfall created strange shadows. Joe lit the path with a flashlight he'd pulled from his Jeep. Linda needed something, too, so she paused and took out a small headlamp. It didn't offer as much light as Joe's, but it helped her avoid hitting her face on branches.

Zero, a dog trained in sunny California, acclimated to the winter conditions with ease. Although there wasn't much call for a tracking dog at the military base, he trained weekly in the skill. He had never done tracking in the snow. Linda wouldn't trust his instincts as an avalanche dog, not with all the training involved, but she was confident he could track a fresh trail no older than two hours, according to the timeline of the teenagers in the house. Zero had followed much older trails when he'd worked as a military police dog. Most days, he handled drug-detection work. That was his best skill set.

Linda often wondered if he hated being confined in Birch Glen without any proper work to do. With her physical therapy and the rehabilitation of her arm, she rarely trained him. This outing was both a treat and a tragedy. That peculiar conflict between doing something you love while dealing with the most difficult days of people's lives was not only limited to the military or police; she'd spoken to firefighters and medical personnel who experienced it too.

Zero continued to lead them farther into the forest, heading down the back of the mountain, past evergreens and over frozen streams. Then the tracks disappeared, but Zero continued to follow the scent from the hidden track.

"I don't get it," Joe said from behind her. "Why would they run away from the house? Are you sure they walked this far?"

"Yes."

He stopped. "No one would randomly walk into the woods like this."

She had to tell him what she suspected, but she hated worrying him further. "Between the timing and location where we started, it looks like they might have witnessed the murder."

Zero pulled the leash, edging to follow the track, but Joe remained frozen in place. "Then they're at risk. We need to locate them immediately. Do you think Payton is involved with these men?"

"I wouldn't assume anything yet. Payton might be an innocent bystander. Give her the benefit of the doubt. From what Natie said, she'd texted them when she arrived at the party, anticipating that Josh would be too drunk to drive home. Aster and Payton could just have been caught at the wrong place but for the right reasons."

"Aster wouldn't have been anywhere near here if she'd remained at home as I'd told her." Joe paused and let out a frustrated moan. "I want to be mad at Aster, but I'm terrified. I won't feel better until I see she's safe."

"My gut tells me she is safe, and until we find her, I'll keep praying that we're guided in the right direction. I think Zero has a good sense of her presence out here. He's focused on the track, and that's a good sign. He tends to lift his head and look around when he loses it or is confused—but we need to move because the snow is not making this easier."

Zero pulled until Linda let him continue moving. He was nose to the ground, only stopping occasionally, then continuing farther away from civilization. Although the search seemed to progress in a definitive direction, Linda worried about the snow and the cold. They had to locate the girls as soon as they could.

Joe had no patience left. He had followed Linda and Zero in the hope the girls would be a hundred yards into the woods, but the trail continued farther and farther away from the Primleys' house. With the snow picking up, he was terrified he'd lose Aster forever.

The wind wasn't helping, sweeping the snow across

the ground and off the pine trees. He'd give anything for a balaclava to protect his neck. The hat he was wearing only came down to protect his ears.

"How are you doing?" Linda asked him.

"I'm feeling unprepared. I was of the assumption the danger for us would be driving off the road, and we'd still have the Jeep with us as a shelter. The last thing I thought was I'd be trekking through the woods."

"I agree. I only grabbed my bag because it held my first aid kit. Luckily, I have a few other things inside that could help if we're forced to build a shelter." Leave it to Linda to carry enough supplies to handle a blizzard.

They paused when Zero gave a low growl. Something large moved ahead of them around the bend. Joe wandered to the side of the path and picked up a large stick. Man or wild animal, he wanted to be prepared.

They continued in silence, Zero leading, but his steps had become more tentative. Linda watched the dog and scanned the area. His head up and ears back, Zero was no longer following the track but had refocused on something else. Joe shadowed them, although he'd feel more confident in protecting Linda if he was up front—not that she seemed in need of much protection.

Linda came to a stop, holding Zero from moving forward. A large crunching on the ground ahead of them stopped him as well. Zero crouched low, pulling the leash taut. A low rumble of a growl came from him.

Their visitor made a few low huffs in reply. The forest at night had all sorts of creatures out and about, but the sounds Joe heard were limited to bears, moose and maybe a coyote. None of those options excited him.

Gripping the long lead tighter, Linda prevented Zero from moving forward. Joe shifted to her side, listening through the wind. Whatever was on the other side of the trees, it stood approximately fifty yards away. Exactly in the direction of Aster's track.

Joe spoke low enough for his voice to blend into the wind. "Did you see what it is?"

"No."

Joe crouched low and peered through the branches. The glow of his flashlight reflected off a wall of dark fur. Zero leaned toward the creature, but Linda dragged him back to her side.

Joe put an arm on her, stopping her from moving forward.

"Do you know what it is?" she whispered.

He took a deep breath. "Bear."

Chapter Seven

Linda didn't want to react in fear over the large, furry animal in front of her, but she'd never encountered a bear so close. While she could philosophize about the bear living in his own environment and being intruded upon by humans, her survival instincts didn't care who had the right-of-way. All she cared about was getting herself, Joe and Zero to safety, then regrouping to follow Aster's track without a bear nearby. They couldn't help anyone if they were smacked down by a three-hundred-pound refrigerator.

The bear, a blanket of black fur against the snow, turned his attention toward them. Closing in at thirty yards, it stepped forward tentatively, huffed and pawed at the ground.

Linda carried a tactical knife with a six-inch blade attached to her pack. If the bear was close enough for her to swipe at it, she was in trouble. The bear's arm span was double hers. The military had trained her to expect anything, and she was decent at hand-to-hand combat, but she'd never practiced against anyone approaching that size.

Zero's growl deepened, and he leaned as far forward on the lead as he could. Linda braced her feet against the snowy ground to keep him from pulling her off balance. "Zero, by me," she ordered, her voice almost a whisper.

The tension eased, and he stepped backward to her side, never letting his focus off the bear. He pressed against her leg. The low rumble of his breathing told her to not let him go—he'd go after the bear and probably lose his life in the process. She couldn't risk it. She knelt closer to him and placed an arm around his neck.

"Easy, boy." She petted the top of his head, assuring both him and herself that everything was going to be okay, even if she wasn't all that certain.

"When I step forward, can you get Zero to bark?" Joe asked.

"You want him to draw the bear's attention?"

"The bear already knows we're here. His nose is better than a dog's."

"Okay. When you give me the word, Zero will bark." She hoped. She'd trained him to bark, but under these circumstances, she had no idea what he'd do or if barking would rile him up enough to pull her right into the bear's vicinity.

"You too. Make a lot of noise." Joe, carrying a large stick, stepped in front of her.

The bear huffed again and advanced toward them. Branches shifted and the monster of an animal pushed its way into their vicinity. She held her breath for a moment, trying to keep the panic inside her.

"Now." Joe rushed forward, waving the stick with one hand and his flashlight with the other, hollering so loud, half the mountain would be able to hear him.

She signaled to Zero to bark as well, which he did with enthusiasm, almost dragging her behind Joe. Then she hollered like Joe had, using as low a voice as she could to avoid sounding like a wounded animal.

Joe aimed his flashlight directly toward the bear. The light had enough lumens to illuminate the whole area. When the beam was directed at the bear's face, it turned away.

They continued the noise until the bear backed down and shuffled away from them, the paw prints so large and recognizable, they could easily avoid following him. Joe stood, facing toward the retreating animal. He was bent over, his hands on his knees.

The sound of branches snapping with the flight of the bear kept Linda frozen in place. Her heartbeat thumped hard across her chest, and she tried to catch her breath as though she'd just run a race. As the sound faded, she could hear her own labored breathing. Zero stared out toward the fading sounds of the bear.

"He seems far away. Are you okay?" He turned and stared into her eyes as if reading whatever lay behind them.

"First bear encounter. Boot camp trained me for a lot of things, but not once did anyone mention how to scare away bears," she answered truthfully.

He pulled her into his arms. The hug drew out the tension that had built up inside her. She rested her head on his shoulder, easing the strain of the moment. The connection with another person—one who had caught her heart once before—melted away the walls she'd built over the years, over the past months. She wanted connection. She wanted connection with him.

She relaxed into his warmth and strength. He fit differently with her than when they'd been in high school together. Despite the thick winter gear, he'd also filled out more—no more tall, lean kid but solid and seemingly immovable. The increased size made her feel safe. He rested his head on top of hers. She could feel the rapid rate of his breathing. He'd rushed the bear to save her. The thought of something going wrong and him being hurt jabbed at her heart in a way that took her off guard.

Zero pulled on the leash, dragging her back from Joe's embrace. She stumbled a bit, then braced her feet. "Zero, easy." Keeping her mind in the right place would ensure they had the best chance of finding Aster, so she calmed the flurry of thoughts rushing through her head and focused on easing the rate of her heartbeat with steady, easy breaths. "I admit, I was frightened, but I was more nervous about you rushing after the bear. And Zero too. He's a clever and strong dog, but at eighty pounds, he's no match for a three-hundred-pound bear."

"True. He did well, though. He remained in control under stressful circumstances. Barking too early might have encouraged the bear. He follows your lead."

"He always has, but he also pushes me at times—enough for him to be effective, especially when I'm ready to turn away from a search and he senses something. Trust is everything between a dog and its handler."

"It's everything between people too." There was untold experience in his words. Now wasn't the time to delve, but being with him these past few hours had made her want to understand more about the choices he'd made in the past and the history he'd lived without her.

She pulled out a few dog treats from her backpack. She always had more snacks for Zero in her pack than for herself. In an emergency, she wouldn't think twice about eating some of the canine peanut butter cookies.

"Sit." She waved a cookie in front of Zero, trying to calm him and reorient his focus from tracking the bear.

He sat and she tossed the treat to him. He caught it and looked right back at her, waiting for more. He'd always been far more food motivated than toy motivated. It made training him easier at times, more difficult at other times. Traveling with a favorite toy instead of a war chest of snacks would be lighter. To make up for the increased snacking, she fed him a better quality of food and used that kibble as additional treats for training instead of feeding him from a bowl. She tossed him another peanut butter cookie, then rubbed his head.

"You're such a good boy. You ready to go back to work?" After so much excitement and confusion, she had to redirect Zero to Aster's trail. He loved to work, so returning his focus to their original task wouldn't be too hard. She backtracked until she found their position from before they'd stopped and fended off the bear. With the snow falling so rapidly and the wind rearranging what was already on the ground, Aster's and Payton's footprints had disappeared. She pulled the freezer bag from her pack and let Zero sniff the baseball hat again. "Where is she, boy? Seek." She pointed to the ground, hoping he'd locate her scent trail again.

He focused on his task as though they'd never encountered the bear. His nose went to the ground, and he started off in a direction. Linda gave him some slack and let him pull her. She couldn't see the footprints under all the snow and was relying entirely on Zero's tracking ability.

The excitement of the past few minutes warmed Linda. She'd felt a chill in her toes and the tips of her fingers as they hiked through the forest, but the extra exertion of her heart pushed blood throughout her limbs, alleviating the sting of the snowy air. She was quite toasty in her jacket and boots, but that would be temporary. Any moisture from the perspiration caused by jumping up and down and yelling would get cold in this temperature, which could increase her risk of hypothermia. If they didn't locate Aster soon, she wasn't sure how much longer into the night they could continue without risking their own health.

They carried on in silence as Zero lead the way. Her confidence in Joe had increased after she'd watched him step forward to scare away the bear. Everyone had their expertise, and Joe was a natural in the wilderness. Not that she should be surprised. Every summer, he and his friends would head out to the forest to climb and hike for a week at a time. In the winter, he'd worked at the ski mountain in exchange for free passes. She glanced back at him. His face had turned crimson red in the cold. His jacket was adequate for a winter hike, as long he kept moving, but his neck had little protection and his gloves weren't nearly warm enough.

They followed Zero under some pine trees that were pressed so close together, the snow remained up on the branches, with little falling to the ground. The sight of footprints in the moist soil under the trees confirmed that Zero had followed the track. They couldn't be that much farther ahead of them. She and Joe pushed through the trees and emerged on a large trail, which stopped them in their tracks. They'd reached a VAST trail. The Vermont Association of Snow Travelers maintained hundreds of miles of snowmobile trails throughout the state. Other, smaller private trails intersected these, making an immense web of destinations possible.

Zero paced around the area, pulling Linda in one direction, then in another. He'd lost their scent. Linda scanned the trail for any footprints, but they were lost in the snow and under recent snowmobile tracks. This could be all for the best if a Good Samaritan had picked up the girls and taken them out of the woods to safety. But the idea that the two men who might have killed Noah had caught up with them hovered over her and wouldn't let go.

"Looks like we lost the scent. They must have gotten on a snowmobile." She examined the area for any sign of them. Two, or possibly three snowmobiles, recently had come through this part of the forest.

Joe stared at the tracks of the snowmobile fading off into the distance. The mountains continued for miles and miles, and the trails curved around them and into the valleys. His arms hung at his sides, and his face lost all expression.

Linda let out a frustrated sigh, powerless to help him. The only thing she could do was manage the search the best she could, allowing Joe the time to process the loss of this opportunity to find his daughter. "I don't know which is better," she said. "We could follow the VAST trail or go back to the Primley place and return with reinforcements. If we can get access to a snowmobile, we could follow much faster."

"We've been hiking for over an hour. Returning will eat up another hour, and we have to drive down the mountain. With the amount of snow coming down, it'll be dangerous." He turned back and forth, his actions mirroring his indecision. "They could be anywhere."

"The kids who left the house should have contacted the police by now. Although I'm sure a bunch of them will be too nervous to get involved, one or two should contact the police. I know the police have satellite phones and radios because of the spotty cellular coverage. They also can put observers at the nearest road crossings."

He shook his head. "If they have the resources for that. You heard your father—they were limited in manpower tonight."

She didn't want to dissuade him, but they had to be reasonable as well. This was not an easy walk in the woods. Already, the effects of the cold were affecting her judgment. It would only get worse as they continued through the night. "The weather is another issue we need to consider before heading farther into the forest. A snowmobile could lead them to someplace warm and dry in a far shorter time than we could walk there."

He stared down at the snowmobile tracks, his shoulders slouched, his expression distant. "Fine. Let's go back and make a new plan. If we have to hike into the woods again, we can bring more appropriate supplies."

"Sounds like the safe thing to do." Linda took a minute to shift her pack to a more comfortable spot resting on her hips and make sure Zero's paws had no snow caught between them. The wax she'd rubbed on them before taking him on the walk in town had protected them from the worst of the cold, although a fitted pair of booties would be better going forward. She'd never thought of him working up here or else she would have outfitted him for the weather. He was her responsibility, and she took that responsibility seriously.

She followed Joe under some pines to return to the trail they'd followed. Before she could tell Joe that Zero would be able to backtrack their own trail to return to the house, she heard a yell and a thud. She ducked under the branches to the edge of a hidden snowy cliff. Joe was nowhere in sight.

Chapter Eight

One second, Joe was crawling under pine boughs, and the next, the earth had disappeared and he tumbled off a cliff hidden by the trees. His head struck a rock jutting out, and he landed on his leg with a thud. The impact punched the wind from his lungs. He lay there, staring up, barely able to see through the snow covering him.

He moved his fingers and toes and rubbed his hand over the spot where his head had struck the rock. He didn't think he'd blacked out, but not remembering a blackout was not an effective way of knowing if he had. There was no blood that he could see and not much discomfort. More painful was the rush of snow up the back of his coat and down his neck. The icy chill brought his body temperature down further. His hat had disappeared somewhere between the top and the bottom of the cliff.

He pushed off the wall of rock and tried to stand. His ankle wouldn't take any weight. His daughter was in danger, and from the pain emanating from his ankle, he'd put his own life at risk—and Linda's as well, if she was forced to slow down to assist him.

"Joe?" Linda's voice fell through the snow and down to where he'd landed.

He could see the outline of her head peering over the ledge. Almost ten feet above him, she appeared like an angel glancing at him from the clouds. Zero stepped cautiously to the edge as well, employing far more caution than Joe had. Because Aster's safety was drowning out his common sense, Joe had rushed ahead, exactly as Linda had told him not to do. The frustration crashed over him. He couldn't rescue his daughter if he himself needed to be rescued.

"Are you hurt?" she called down to him.

"I twisted my ankle, but I'm fine." The injury wasn't going to stop him from finding Aster.

"Is it broken?" she asked.

"I don't think so." He reached down and rubbed up and down his leg. He could move his foot without too much pain. Bracing his feet in the snow, he forced himself through the sharp pain to a standing position. He could push himself a few feet, but they must have walked over a mile into the forest. Now wasn't the time to fake bravado, not if it could slow Linda down and create a bad situation for her too. "I might need some help."

"I'm going to find a safer path down to you. Try not to move too much."

He wasn't going far. He leaned against the rocky wall and lifted the weight off his bad leg. Wind gusted through the area, taking the last of the light with it. He couldn't waste time, not when his daughter was out there somewhere with a murderer. Frustrated with the situation, he tried to take a step, but pain shot through his ankle, doubling him over.

When Linda arrived, she tied Zero's leash to a nearby tree and went to Joe's side. She bent over and pulled his knit hat out of the snow. "What happened? I heard you fall but didn't see it. Did you hit your head?" Her hand reached out and brushed away the snow that was pressed into the opening of his shirt at his neck and some in his hair. Her fingers traced light pressure over his scalp as she looked for injuries, but her touch also eased the heavy strain pressing into him, crushing him under guilt and fear. Her fingers rested on the side of his head. "There's a little bump behind your ear. It's not cut, but it's something we need to be aware of."

She scanned his eyes—looking for signs of a head injury, perhaps—then directed her headlamp at them to get a better look. He blinked at the brightness. When the light dropped away from his face, they were face-to-face. Their lips were a mere inch away from a kiss. He remembered how sweet she tasted when he'd kissed her in high school. Somehow, in the middle of a storm crashing through his life, all he wanted was to hide out for a few moments in that sweetness. Her hand caressed his cheek, and she rested her forehead on his, as though holding herself back from the same memories.

A crush of cold swirled between them, breaking the moment. She sat back, away from him. "Looks okay so far, but I'm no medical expert." Her voice was muted by the storm.

"As long as we can manage a way out of here and find Aster."

She reached into her backpack and pulled out a large plastic bag and a space blanket. That thing was more useful than Mary Poppins's carpet bag. "Let's shift you onto this bag. It'll keep you from getting wet, and I'll wrap you with the blanket until I can figure how to evacuate you."

"'Evacuate'?"

She placed the bag on the ground and guided Joe into a seated position. "I don't see you walking all the way out of here right now. We need to stabilize your ankle and make sure your head injury is not worse than it looks."

"My head feels okay." But he couldn't deny that his left ankle was a mess. There was a sense of embarrassment and vulnerability, sitting on the ground in front of his former girlfriend. She remained focused on assisting him. As their situation grew more and more perilous, she became calmer and more fixed on handling things one step at a time. After a few minutes, he let go of any childish pretense about him having to be the strong one. She had her expertise, and he had his own. After all, he had run the bear off.

"I'm okay to walk out. I just need a strong stick to help me." But he wasn't really okay. If Aster had been safe back at the inn, he'd never attempt to walk out, but as long as she was missing, he had to carry on.

"Maybe, but let me look at it first."

She lifted his foot, still secured in its boot, and turned it slightly until he winced. She then placed her hand on the sole of the boot and asked him to push. He could barely move the palm of her hand without his face giving away his discomfort.

She shook her head. "I don't know if you have a fracture, but it's at least a bad sprain. Walking on it could make it worse." Her expression darkened. "With your wet clothes and these injuries, you need to shelter for a bit. I don't think trying to push through will benefit anyone."

The snowfall had increased over the past few minutes, creating whiteout conditions that made hiking even more dangerous. Each step forward created more and more obstacles toward getting to Aster.

"I don't care. I have to get moving." He'd already wasted so much time, and they were backtracking.

Linda took out several rolls of tape from her first aid kit. His own first aid kit sat in the Jeep. He'd never been so unprepared, and admittedly, without Linda by his side, he might have made choices that would have put himself and maybe Aster in an even more perilous situation.

She lifted his foot with a gentleness and placed it on her lap, removing his boot. She used both hands to rub the foot to warm it and feel for any injury, an examination that resembled a mini massage, with pressure in the arch of his foot and the tension of her fingers pressing deep toward the bone. Her fingers lingered on the bottom of his feet, alleviating the strain on his heel, and rubbed the arch until the muscles in his foot relaxed and the pain eased. Then she wrapped the tape from his heel to his shin and around his ankle. She continued until he couldn't rotate his foot side to side. His trainer from when he had played football had secured his ankle in much the same way.

"This a compression wrap, to prevent swelling with some limited stability for your ankle. Under the circumstances, we should try to head back to the house. If it's too much, tell me." She loosened the laces of his boot and slipped it back on. It hurt more than he cared to admit. She tightened it enough to keep the boot from coming off as he walked.

If Linda hadn't accompanied him, he'd be in much worse shape. It was as though she'd stood on the roadside in Birch Glen just to help him. Not that he believed God was working on his side, but maybe—just maybe—He had sent an angel to assist him out of pity.

He tried to stand, his arm wrapped over her shoulder. She was strong and helped him to his feet, but any pressure on that foot sent jagged chills straight through his leg. He took a strangled breath and a step. His daughter needed him, and he wasn't going to spend the night in the woods while someone took her farther away from him.

"How does it feel?" she asked.

"I'm good," he said, sucking up the pain.

"Are you sure?" she asked, her voice laced with skepticism.

He didn't reply.

They had to get back to the Primley place and his car. As Linda folded up the plastic bag and space blanket and unclipped Zero's leash from the tree, Joe attempted a few more steps, holding the side of the cliff for support. He inhaled sharply at the pain. He stepped again, almost buckling to the ground, and nearly cursed out the whole world at his situation.

He'd risk permanent damage to his leg to save Aster. Heck, he'd give pretty much everything he had for her safety. Linda came back over to him and guided him several steps, and Zero pulled them both, absorbing some of the energy it took to work their way back up the slope. They climbed up an easier path than he'd fallen down, but now that they weren't tucked into the protection of the cutout in the mountain, a gust of wind nearly sent them tumbling back over the edge. He stumbled to the ground. He stood again and took a few more steps. The harsh wind burned his cheeks. The blizzard conditions came at them with a brutal force.

"I can't see anything," Linda called out to him over the whistling cry of the wind.

Visibility had dropped to several feet, and without adequate gear, the risk of frostbite grew. As the temperature fell, the risks increased exponentially. Hypothermia could kill them both before they arrived back at the house. The weather in the Green Mountains had killed many people who had underestimated the cold. Joe not only had Aster to worry about but Linda as well.

Another gust of wind sent a flurry of snow cascading over him from a nearby pine tree and pushed him over again.

The anger that bubbled inside him let loose. "Why are you doing this to me?" he screamed toward the sky. "I can't handle it anymore. Stop. Please, stop." He clenched his fists, overwhelmed and unsure of anything.

Linda walked over to him. "We're going to find her."

"You can't be sure of that."

"We can't be sure of anything, but if we keep doing our best, things will work out. Have faith."

He shook his head. He'd been told to have faith over and over again, only to watch those he loved suffer around him. "I had faith that Ivy would be around to help raise Aster. I had faith that my mother would survive the stroke that took her life. I'm trying to have faith in finding Aster, but how many mountains do I need to climb to prove I'm worthy?"

"Worthy of what? You're a compassionate man who works hard and cares about not only his family but this town as well. I'm sorry for everything that hit you in life, but standing still in a blizzard isn't going to bring them back or help us find Aster. We need to move to a safer space." She hooked her arm through his, her steadiness pulling him back together.

They hiked about fifty yards. She assisted him to a row of pines that blocked the heavy impact of the wind and provided a more comfortable spot to rest. After tying Zero under the branches to keep him drier, she took off her pack, then laid out the plastic bag on the ground again and hustled around, leaving Joe sitting, useless. He moved himself and the bag farther out of the wind and snow.

Within the next hour, she had stacked a few pine boughs from surrounding trees to increase their protection from the snow and wind, started a small fire, and given Joe some pain medication to help reduce the swelling in his ankle.

"You're quite the Boy Scout," he said, trying to lower the tension he'd tossed toward her in his earlier break-down.

"*Girl* Scout. I picked up some pretty cool patches in first aid and wilderness survival but was horrible at sell-ing cookies. Too bad—sales and marketing skills can add up to a successful life in today's world."

"I'm not sure sales or marketing would be much help tonight."

"True. My years in the marines added to my Girl Scout survival skills. If I could survive the Crucible, I could survive anything. Although, to be fair, it wasn't this cold on Parris Island." She sat with him by the fire. It was the first time she'd sat in one spot for more than a minute or two. Unlike a lot of the workaholics he knew—including himself—there was a stillness within Linda at rest. Zero had curled into her side, and she stared out at the fire, her fingers rubbing behind the ears of the content dog.

The moment didn't last long enough. She stood up. "Okay, let's take care of that ankle so we can get out of here easier in a few hours, after the storm passes."

Hours? "We're staying all night?" They had to leave and find Aster.

"I don't think we have a choice. I won't risk your or Zero's safety."

"What about yours?"

A wistful expression passed over her features. "I like to think that being one of the two survivors of the heli-copter crash, I have a special purpose on Earth."

"To save ex-boyfriends?" He smiled, needing to ease the strain that she seemed to be trying to hide.

"Among other things." She helped him into a more comfortable position, elevated his ankle and placed some snow on the swollen area, although he was so cold already, he didn't see the point.

After she wrapped him again with the space blanket, she shifted closer to the fire, warming her fingers. "Hungry?"

"Let me guess: you have a freeze-dried lasagna and blueberry cobbler in your pack."

"I wish. How about a few energy bars and some water?"

"I'll take it."

Linda could feel Joe's frustration. She had no solution for his inability to walk except to rest for a few hours and carry on at first light. She couldn't carry him out of the forest in blizzard conditions. Being such a big guy, she could barely assist him in decent weather. Over six feet tall, he'd always laughed at their height difference. When they'd danced at the prom together, her arms couldn't wrap around his neck without him bending forward. Thinking back to high school sent waves of memories rushing over her. Moments of holding hands in a rainstorm; laughing at his impression of the principal ordering everyone back into class after a fire drill; watching him throw the ball to the wide receiver in the end zone and sending the crowd into chaos; walking away from him, tears in her eyes, her heart breaking with each step she took.

She handed him some pain medicine, a granola bar and some water. His skin appeared too pale, his hair damp from his fall. His wet hat had been placed close to the fire to dry. He needed something warmer. She took off her hat and gave it to him. Her jacket had a hood she could wear.

Holding the white knit hat with the large white pom-pom in his hand, he rolled his eyes. "This is embarrassing. I'm fine, Linda."

"It's the little things that make a difference. My hood is fine for me, but you're losing far too much heat. I refuse to have you wear a soaking-wet hat when mine will be much warmer." In the darkness, by the fire, in the middle of a storm, her thoughts went off in strange directions. For the first time since she'd arrived back in Birch Glen, she wasn't obsessing about her own issues. Instead, she was focused on making sure Joe would make it through the night so they could then find Aster and Payton. "Just humor me for tonight and tell me I overreacted when we're both drinking coffee at the café tomorrow."

He put on the hat, then took a bite of the energy bar. "I might have a stack of Molly's pancakes with my coffee too."

"With the warmed maple syrup and butter." She savored the sweet flavors flooding her imagination.

"Exactly." A smile brightened his face as though he, too, were enjoying a meal from his past. "Now I'm starving."

"I've got you covered."

When she reached out to give him another energy

bar, he held her hand. The touch charged the space with a different type of heat. A whole lot of *what if*s swirled over her, but she released them in exchange for *what is*. She was next to the man she'd always loved, even when she didn't want to, and he needed her. It wasn't the whirlwind romantic reunion of movies, but having him back in her life for even a few moments felt right, even if their paths would never cross again when all this was over and her life took her somewhere new.

"Did you ever date anyone else after me?" he asked.

"I lived." She refused to hand over a play-by-play recap of her few relationships while in the military. The men she'd dated were hardworking, handsome and funny, but they weren't Joe. "But I never met anyone I wanted to spend the rest of my life with."

He nodded. "I'm sorry for the injury that ended your career, but I'm glad you're back."

"Thanks."

His fingers relaxed, and exhaustion took hold of him. Rest, water and food would be best for them both.

Hunger plagued her, too, as her body warmed by the fire. Her bag contained a few random energy bars, dog treats, water in Nalgene containers and a collapsible silicon dog bowl. She also had some herbal tea bags left over from a camping trip the summer before her accident. She really needed to update her supplies when they got back to town. Not that she could complain. She had supplies, and had she not grabbed her pack on the way to the Primleys' house, they'd be in a far more dangerous situation. As it was, she could only hope his head injury wasn't a concussion or worse and that his ankle injury wasn't a fracture. She moved closer to him and checked the bump on his head, her fingers brushing over his skin. He was still too cold, and she was running out of supplies.

Some tea would warm him up, but she had nothing to heat the water with. She went through her pack again and poured Zero some water in his bowl. He slopped it up and looked at her for more. "Sorry, fella, we need to ration the supplies."

She passed Joe the water container to keep him from getting dehydrated and looked at Zero's empty bowl. Silicon. She could heat water in it and make tea for Joe. It wasn't ideal but would work in a pinch. This certainly qualified as being in a pinch. She rubbed Zero's head and took the bowl from him. She filled it with snow to clean it, then used her sleeve to wipe it out. Not the most sterile cleaning, but the heat would kill off most of the remaining germs.

"What are you doing?" he asked.

"I'm making us tea."

"In that?"

"Unless you brought a small pan with you, yes."

She placed a large rock from next to the trunk of one of the pines in the middle of the fire and sat the bowl filled with water on top of it. "Hopefully, that will be enough to make us some hot water."

"I don't know what I would have done without you. I never rush into the wilderness without supplies, and here you are, saving me."

"You had other things to think about. Probably why

doctors rarely treat their own family members. Too much emotion involved."

The wind continued to howl, and the snow swirled around their makeshift shelter. Zero snuggled into her. His presence both warmed and calmed her. She'd never owned a dog growing up but found life impossible without them after joining the canine unit of the military police. Her first working dog, a sweet yellow lab named Jelly, was living the beach life in San Diego with a retired sergeant. Although Linda missed her, Jelly provided warmth and stability to her current human companion, a man Linda respected for the way he'd dealt with the hardships of a post-military life. The new assignment also gave Jelly a much-needed purpose after spending years on the job. Zero was Linda's second operational dog and had been with her since he'd arrived on base as a feisty ten-month-old puppy. By then, he'd passed through multiple evaluations and received basic training. The trainers had wanted an experienced handler for him, and she volunteered. He'd been a handful, always pushing the limits, but his enthusiasm for the work turned him from disobedient adolescent to a first-rate working dog. They'd instantly bonded, working hours each day to get him ready to certify. Zero was a natural at narcotics detection. His nose could find trace amounts of drugs that other dogs passed over. He'd once located a stash of heroin behind the dry wall in a soldier's apartment, and soon after, he and Linda were assisting in searches on other military bases. Everything had been perfect until the accident. After the crash, he'd refused to go near a helicopter, but that was part of their job, as they often traveled up and down the coast in the quickest means possible. Linda couldn't convince the military higher-ups that besides his aversion to helicopters, he was still 100 percent capable.

They'd been brushed aside. She'd held on to a lot of hostility for being removed from what she loved. After finding such a fulfilling career and then losing it, she'd lost her identity for a time. The months of physical therapy had restored her body, and a psychologist had taught her how to deal with the internal trauma. She was more than ready to return to service, but the idea of leaving Zero behind didn't sit right with her. They were a team, and perhaps she was acting unprofessional by refusing to return without him, but she couldn't see life without her best friend.

When the water came to a boil, she used her Leatherman pliers to pull the bowl from the fire. The outside of the bowl had turned black with soot, but the inside remained clear enough. When she added the peppermint tea, the aroma of mint brought a sense of well-being to a treacherous situation. She glanced over at Joe: he'd fallen asleep. After she'd received a head injury a few years back in a base soccer game, her doctor had told her the old adage of waking someone every two hours when they had a concussion was no longer followed. She heeded his advice and let Joe sleep. She'd keep an eye on him, but the rest would help them more than her waking him up all night. Tomorrow would be a difficult day. She sent Zero over to him to provide additional warmth. Zero complied, curling up next to him as though they had been best buddies forever. Between the dog, the fire and the space blanket, Joe had enough protection to keep Linda from fearing hypothermia. The risk still remained but to a lesser degree.

She sipped the tea and stared at the man she'd once thought of as the person she'd love forever. A wisp of his dark hair curled from under her hat. He'd been cute as a high school senior, but he'd grown into his chiseled features. More rugged, more handsome, with a depth of emotion he'd never revealed back when they'd dated. He wore the title of *father* well. His love for Aster showed in every action he took, and that vulnerability broke down whatever remaining anger had lingered within her at his reaction to her leaving home after high school.

A barrel full of *what if*s swirled through her mind. What if she'd never enlisted in the marines? What if she'd remained in Birch Glen? What if he'd never married Ivy? But *what if*s were best left in the past. Everything that had happened from yesterday and before offered lessons on moving forward, but those memories shouldn't be barriers to living fully.

Her years in the military had forged her with self-reliance, confidence and the mental strength to make it through tough situations. She wouldn't be this version of Linda Jameson if she'd stayed, and she liked this version. When she'd first enlisted, she was convinced it had been a mistake. Always last in the run around the camp; failing the simplest tasks, such as making her bed and folding her clothes. And despite years of practice with her father, she'd been an absolute embarrassment at the gun range. The blisters on her feet and the strain in her muscles had hit her with a mountain of self-doubt, but somewhere toward the end of her thirteen weeks of boot camp, something clicked. The daily regimen had started making sense, and she'd begun to excel.

She wouldn't have been a dog mom to Jelly and Zero if she'd deleted the past decade. No, it was for the best that she'd left Birch Glen. If only her confidence from the marines had traveled back to Birch Glen with her. After months of being unemployed, she hadn't accomplished anything worthwhile since returning to her parents' house. She woke up, did physical therapy and walked her dog. There had to be something more that would give her a purpose—and if not here, then elsewhere.

After what felt like only a few minutes, Zero shifted in his sleep and pushed his paws into the side of her leg. He was out, but Joe was awake and watching her. He was mindlessly rubbing Zero's back. His stress level and frustration seemed to have dissipated some after his short rest. That would only help them in the long run. They needed to be strong mentally and physically, and with his ankle, head injury and the cold, they were already encumbered physically.

Linda refilled the bowl and placed it back on the rock in the fire. "How are you feeling?"

He shrugged. "My ankle hurts, my back is wedged into a stick of some sort and I want to wring the neck of the guy who shot Noah."

She nodded and lifted the bowl off the fire when the first bubbles appeared. "Tea?"

"Please." He took the bowl from her. "Peppermint? It reminds me that it's already December twenty-third. Only two more days to Christmas. Only a few hours ago, all I cared about was the success of the inn, even to the detriment of my own family."

"When you bought the inn, it was an eyesore. Your vision made it not only beautiful but also a reason to come and stay in Birch Glen. You're sort of a town hero. I bet Aster's proud of her father. I would be."

He shrugged in response.

She wouldn't convince him of his parenting skills while Aster was out there at risk, so she changed the subject. "I was thinking we could rest for a few hours, then push on. I know you're upset about being delayed, but there's a reason for everything."

"That's such a stupid saying."

"It is?"

"There was a reason for Ivy dying? A reason for my father to beat my mother? A reason for my mother's miserable death? A reason for the helicopter to crash and all those people to die except you?"

"Said like that, it does sound pretty lame. Maybe there is no reason—although I prefer to believe the world isn't as cruel as it sometimes appears. Maybe we need to have faith."

"Honestly, I just want to finish this tea and sleep. Don't push your optimism toward me. I have real-life issues that have to be resolved, and the only thing that will solve them are hard work and luck."

She remained silent after that. She certainly didn't want to upset him. Life hadn't been easy for him, and he had every reason in the world to be bitter. Looking out toward the snow and wind, she prayed for some light to fall over him.

* * *

Joe let the tea warm his insides and silently acknowledged that Linda had been right: the rest had made a difference by giving him warmth and, he hoped, strength. Despite the storm raging around them, she had located a relatively dry spot that was tucked out of the wind, flat and more than sufficient under the circumstances. Even the small fire she fed to keep them warm was what was needed to ward off the worst effects of the biting cold. If it wasn't for her, his fingers, toes and even the tip of his nose would be at risk for frostbite. Instead, he was bundled up and—if not warm, exactly—more comfortable than he would have been farther out in the elements. If only she wasn't so excessively hopeful. Handling reality required more than a prayer.

Zero shifted next to him, his big head resting on his leg. For a dog who had walked through a snowstorm, he threw off a serious amount of heat. Joe appreciated the extra warmth and looked over at Linda. She had to be cold sitting a few steps closer to the opening, but she never complained. He watched her add a few branches she'd picked up from under the pines, keeping the heat consistent. Then she brushed herself off, stepped into the clearing and rolled several large snowballs. More like snow boulders.

"Strange time to be making a snowman," he said.

"It's Christmas. I'm being festive."

"Really?"

She laughed. "No. I'm making a sort of igloo using the snow for one wall and the pine trees for the other."

She pushed one of the snowballs right up to the edge

of the pine tree they were under. Again and again, she pushed heavy clumps of snow, building a wall of snow, leaving a space for the fire and a small entrance. The temperature rose quickly with the space protected on almost all four sides.

"Clever. But I'd brush away some of the pine needles on the floor to make it a less flammable."

She glanced around and nodded. "I didn't think of that, but I agree." She made quick work of the loose needles near the fire, leaving a ring of snowy dirt to buffer the area.

When she finished, she squeezed next to Zero, who had spread out across where she'd sat before the construction of their shelter. He leaned his head on her leg. She deserved the extra warmth for all the work she'd accomplished. Joe shifted his arm toward her and gestured for her to use it as a pillow. She did. Her head rested in a perfect spot on his shoulder; his arm held her tight. They turned to each other, their faces only inches away. Her cheeks were red from all the effort she'd put in in the storm.

"Are you cold?" he asked.

"Not too bad. The work gave me a needed temperature boost, but I probably will be soon."

He tightened his arm around her. It felt different to hold her after years and years apart. He'd been too preoccupied with feeling sorry for himself and jealous of her chance to leave Birch Glen even to attempt keeping their relationship going. Although, truth be told, he'd been focused more on his physical attraction to her, failing to appreciate her strength, thoughtfulness and honesty. By not seeing her as a person with her own dreams and ambitions, he missed some of the best parts of her. He wanted more details on the people she'd dated. From what people in town had said, there might have been someone a few years back, but she was single now. Could he bring that up? Did he want to know the answer?

He stared at her, her face illuminated in the firelight. Her presence so close to him eased his stress. Her appearance in town had been oddly comforting to him, as though an old friend had returned, even if they hadn't spoken except for the occasional greeting before today. Perhaps she'd stick around for a while longer. She'd be a wonderful role model for Aster, if they could spend time together. He swallowed hard. He had to believe that he'd see them together, but he couldn't help his daughter if he was out of commission, so he took a few deep breaths and tried to rest. He closed his eyes, asking God for something positive, something to give him hope.

Chapter Nine

The orange rays of the sun breaking above the horizon woke Joe. He stretched and looked over at Linda, but she wasn't there. He sat up. The walls of snow still stood with several inches of additional powder, and the fire smoldered, keeping their makeshift shelter at a survivable temperature. He heard movement outside. Zero was in the snow, on his back and wiggling side to side, his tail wagging, his tongue hanging out his mouth. When he finished, he popped onto four paws and shook, bits of snow flying off his fur. He paused and looked around until his big brown eyes landed on Joe. In a burst of energy, Zero sprinted toward him. Joe braced for the worst.

"Down," Linda called out.

Zero dropped to his belly a few feet before coming into contact.

"Sorry, he just had a bit of playtime chasing some snowballs while I scouted the area. He reverts to crazy-puppy mode when he plays." She arrived with fresh wood and added it to the fire. "How is your ankle?"

He flexed it as best as he could with her wrapping still holding it. "I won't know until I put pressure on it again, but so far, so good."

Zero remained in down position, his tail wagging, ready to pounce. Linda pointed to a fairly dry spot under the tree. "Go over there."

Zero followed her directions and moved away from them, stretching out on the ground.

"I heated some tea for you with the same tea bag from last night. It won't be as strong, but there's some taste." She handed him the bowl and pulled out another power bar. "Last one, so we should move out this morning. Can you walk in this snow? It's much deeper than last night."

He flexed his ankle again and winced at the still-throbbing pain. "I can make it," he insisted. "If I take my time." Although time was the main thing lacking in his life.

They spent the next few minutes packing. He tended to whatever he could reach from his spot on the mat. Linda folded the makeshift blankets and stowed them back in her pack.

When she'd left for the marines, he'd been devastated. As much as he wanted her by his side, he knew she'd never be happy if she stayed. Not that she could have stayed. She'd signed away her life for several years, and a brokenhearted boyfriend wasn't enough to break the terms. In hindsight, ghosting her had hurt them both. Had he just been honest with her, they might have retained their bond.

His relationship with Ivy had helped heal his heartache. He'd truly cared for her. She'd added color to his life and stood by his side as his mother's health deteriorated. Marrying her quickly so his mother could be at the wedding was his gift to the woman who had sacrificed so much for him. Ivy hadn't been a mistake; she'd been a blessing at a time when Joe didn't see anything positive in the world. She wore a smile that set the world on fire and had a generosity for anyone in need. And she was the mother of his child. His chest tightened. Ivy's death haunted him, and her ghost followed him through the forest, scolding him for Aster's situation. He had to get their daughter back. Despite all the conflict he and Aster had experienced, he couldn't imagine a day in his life without her: mornings without fighting for the last of the Froot Loops, rainy days spent watching *Law & Order: SVU* and arguing over the outcomes, pizza with green peppers and pineapple on Friday nights. Except he'd been too busy last night.

After he bundled up for the colder air outside this protected space, he stood on his good foot. Tentatively, he placed his left foot to the ground. It still hurt, but with the snow pack on it overnight and additional medicine from Linda, he could walk better than several hours before. He'd be fine. Aster's safety was not so certain. He had no idea where to look for her and what the motive was for her and Payton to run.

"Ready to go?" Linda asked, lifting her pack onto her back. "The snow stopped, the wind's down and the sun's coming up. It should be much more comfortable to hike today."

"I'm in your debt. My ankle can take more weight on it than it could have last night. I might be sore for a week or two, but for the next few hours, I should be fine." He shifted closer to the fire and dropped snow on the embers to put it out.

"Great. Have you set your intentions for today or said a quick prayer?"

He grumbled. "I want Aster back, that's all."

She ignored his response. "I prayed that we'd have a better idea of Aster's location in the daylight."

He couldn't take any false hope. He didn't want to believe things would get better and then be let down again. "And did God send you a sign? An arrow in the sky, pointing down to the exact spot she's at right now?" He immediately regretted his harsh words. Taking out his anger on Linda wouldn't help anything. He was still unsure of what he believed, despite his own silent prayers. "God and I haven't had been on speaking terms for a few years."

She placed a light hand on his shoulder. "Neither have we, but look at what happens when you let someone in. You get a friend." She squeezed his arm and smiled.

He couldn't help but feel more positive being near her, but the anxiety hovering over him shifted his thoughts back to Aster. He stared at the miles of space in front of them. His daughter was who-knows-where by now. "So did you hear back from God on Aster's location?" he asked with an edge.

She looked over her shoulder toward the mountainous terrain. "I think so. Whatever it is, it's a good distance from here but seems closer than the Primleys' house."

"What did you see?"

She pointed to a low spot halfway up the next mountain. Barely visible, a plume of smoke snaked toward the sky from between a thick clump of trees.

He took in a deep breath of air. A sign of life in the middle of nowhere, but the location wasn't accessible by any roads he knew of. "I agree. We should go there."

Linda nodded. "Are you okay walking through the snow?"

"I have to be." He took a few steps, tentative at first, but then found a stride that could support him.

"Zero and I will break the path through the snow so you have less work to do with your ankle."

They left their camp and ventured toward the area where the smoke could be seen, their movements softened by the fresh snow. Joe took one slow step at a time. They remained close together but silent. The path wasn't as easy as the one they'd followed the night before from the Primleys' house.

Zero led them, pulling at the lead, sniffing the air and the ground. The deep snow made travel for him difficult as well. Every few moments, he turned back to Linda, and she'd make a subtle flick of her hand for him to turn and carry on. Their connection was something that didn't require loud commands or punishments when Zero acted up. They communicated through their body language and by checking in with each other: Linda, always the leader; Zero, reacting to her cues. Joe could see how they made a solid team. There was an abundance of trust between them.

At one point, as they hiked under a large stand of

trees, they lost sight of the smoke. Linda stopped. When Joe came up to her, he saw a compass in her hand.

She pointed toward the peak of a mountain just over the tree line. "If we continue west toward the ridge, we should find the source of the smoke."

They traveled farther to a break in the trees. The terrain was unsteady, but Joe saw the smoke again, still beckoning him and Linda toward it. Perhaps to find Aster, to locate an easier way off the mountain or to a radio to connect with outside help. An incredibly lucky discovery. He ignored the voice inside guiding him forward, offering assistance. Something deeper calling to him.

His ankle still ached, but he didn't need to lean on Linda to walk. That allowed them both to move quicker. If he could find a way to take some of the pressure off it and give him more stability, he'd be able to go farther, faster. When they came to a large downed tree with several limbs broken on the ground and dusted over with snow, he looked over the offerings. Most branches were too short or thin to be useful for anything more than firewood, but there was one larger branch, about five feet tall, wide enough to hold his weight. It made the perfect walking stick.

He dismissed the thought that the branch was perfect for him and was in his path due to a great plan. It was lucky. Although Joe had never been lucky in the past. Except in his business. Somehow, everything worked out at the inn even when things looked impossible. He'd found an exceptionally capable and trustworthy team who worked to make the inn a jewel in the valley. He also had located outside suppliers that eased his work-load and made the operation less stressful, including the laundromat, the baker and even the bank. He believed in the inn, and things had come together. He could in-vest that same amount of faith in other things—more important things, like his daughter.

He thought of Linda—out of a job and injured yet still believing life would work out for her. Had she fallen apart the night before, he would have been in trouble. She'd been the stability that helped him through. A thought occurred to him: once he had Aster back, per-haps he could convince Linda to try small-town life again. Not that they knew much about each other since high school, but if she remained in town, they'd have a chance to perhaps rekindle something that had once been there. The concept sounded perfect in theory, but she had her own plans. She wanted to return to work. No military bases were located close by, so she'd prob-ably end up a few hundred miles away. The idea de-pressed him.

Linda stopped ahead. He joined her. The weather was better today than it had been yesterday. He allowed the rays of the sun to warm his face. Every bit of warmth helped since he had never fully thawed out from the night before.

"I don't know if we're going to be welcome where we're headed, so it would be best to tread softly and learn as much as we can before asking for coffee and a place by the fire." She gestured to Zero. He leaped up and down to get over the snow drifts and then sat by her side, his tail wagging as though sitting next to her was the best treat possible.

Joe nodded. "I agree. Do you want to split up?"

She paused at that. "The more we're apart, the more footprints we'll leave in the snow, even in snow this deep. I think it would be better to stick together and avoid the main pathways up to the cabin. I'm still worried about your ankle too. I know it's working right now, but that doesn't mean you're ready for an all-day hike in the snow."

"I'm fine." He continued toward the smoke. The walking stick, the tea and the pain medicine he'd taken earlier helped drive him forward. He had to be okay. Aster was counting on him.

Chapter Ten

After several minutes, they intersected with the snow-mobile trail. The snow was more packed down, but with a fresh cover of snow, their footprints stood out, announcing their arrival to anyone who saw them.

"We need to stay off the path."

She nodded. "How's your ankle?"

"It hates me, but it won't stop me."

To his left, he saw something sticking up from the snow. Red fabric.

"Wait," he called out to Linda, pointing to the anomaly.

She remained where she was, and he moved forward tentatively. He pulled it out: a red knit mitten. He flipped it over and saw something that added layers of excitement and fear to an already overflowing bucket of emotions. There was a heart embroidered into the palm of the mitten. It was Aster's mitten. He'd given them to her on Christmas the year before. It was a one-of-a-kind pair of mittens made by Terry O'Donnell, the founder of the local artisan cooperative. Joe had asked her for something special for Aster. Terry made the mittens red to symbolize Aster's joie de vivre, and the heart was placed on the palms so everything Aster touched would be filled with love. It was kind of corny, but Aster loved them.

He shook his head at the discovery. His throat tightened. Aster couldn't be far from here. It wasn't until Linda was by his side and she placed her hands on his shoulders, trying to calm him down and keep his movements quieter, that he realized how distressed he'd become.

"What did you find?" she asked.

"Aster's mitten." He held it up. "It's hers. I gave them to her."

"Believe it or not, that's a good sign. It says we're moving in the right direction. We need to stay focused."

Joe nodded. He pulled out his phone and the map app.

"What are you doing? Do you have service?"

"No, but I'm marking this spot on my phone. The GPS navigation works independently from the data connection. Usually."

She pulled her phone out too. The battery was dead. "Can you try texting the data to someone who checks their phone often? If we happen to have even a moment of connectivity, the text may go through."

"Good idea. Why didn't you do that last night?"

"I didn't think of it. I think the bear knocked my good sense out of me."

"Without you, I'd be a snowman right now. You had enough sense to keep me alive." He meant it. Had it not been for her survival skills, he might have succumbed to hypothermia on the long trek back.

They continued hiking. A somberness cast over their trek. The people they were chasing were dangerous and perhaps panicked. Men pushed into corners didn't act rationally and, in this case, could be downright deadly.

The smell of a fireplace propelled them to move at a quicker pace. He placed the mitten in his pocket and allowed the need to see his daughter shield him from the pain in his ankle, the cold around him, the fear in his heart and the image of Noah shot dead on the ground.

Linda and Zero moved slow enough to keep Joe, hobbling behind them, within their view. After a year spent on asphalt sidewalks and in physical therapy, Linda's feet were sore. She hadn't hiked so far in a long time. Not since before she'd been in the accident. If no one was at the cabin, they'd be forced to remain there for a bit to warm up and rest for the long hike out, but she was confident someone was coming. Either the students would report them missing or her father would notice she hadn't come home. Although, looking at the amount of snow that fell, their rescue might be delayed.

"We're almost there. I can smell the smoke," she said. Although the scent often reminded her of a comfortable evening reading a book and drinking hot tea, today the scent had an acrid edge. The source might be a gunman's lair, not a place to find rest and nourishment.

A small wooden cabin came into view, the type of structure hikers would use to spend the night off the frozen trail. A simple four-wall, single-floor and probably one-room dwelling with small windows, a stone chimney and a porch no bigger than ten feet wide. Enough of a shelter to get out of the rain or snow and have a warm place to spend a night. There were many of these cabins up here, some set up by the national park and others remnants of an earlier time. Someone took care of this one. A pile of firewood had been stacked inside a small open shed to the side of the cabin, keeping the wood dry and available no matter the weather. The two front windows had a frosty covering so they wouldn't be able to see inside.

There were several sets of footprints, mostly covered in snow, so they couldn't make out the shoe sizes from where they were standing at the wood line to where the footprints were located by the stairs of the cabin. Linda crouched behind several fir trees. Zero stood at her side. He shifted occasionally but otherwise remained still. The focus he had when working had always impressed her. It was as though he could read her emotions to determine when to rush forward and when to settle into silence. He never complained, neither a whimper nor a whine when he was tired, hungry or they needed to get moving. Zero understood his job and performed it no matter what. The conditions could involve below-freezing weather and hurricane winds, and Zero would still be the first out the door to go to work. She rubbed her hand behind his ears. He looked up at her, then looked back toward Joe, who arrived a few minutes after her.

They stared at the cabin. Based on the location of Aster's mitten and the two snowmobiles parked outside, there was a decent chance Aster and Payton were inside. There had to be a way to get them out without putting them at risk. They could wait until someone emerged from the cabin. Yet there was a chance that if they waited too long, something bad would happen inside—if it hadn't already. The thought twisted Linda's insides. She knew Joe had been upset about spending the night instead of pushing on, but they would have had an impossible time following the track in the storm. Instead, he'd rested his ankle and they'd located the smoke that led them here. In fact, they'd probably cut off two miles of snowmobile trails by hiking directly toward the cabin instead of relying on the trail. Linda watched Joe's stricken face. He'd been through so much, and locating Aster's mitten would only fuel his anxiety about his daughter, but he had to remain levelheaded, both for Aster's safety and theirs.

Linda leaned closer to Joe. "We need to back up, away from the line of sight. Our best weapon aside from Zero is surprise."

He nodded and they moved behind another row of trees that provided a decent vantage point to observe what was going on at the cabin but wouldn't expose their location. If only they could see inside.

Zero stood at Linda's side; he had less of the high drive he'd shown the night before when pulling Linda along Aster's track. His mannerisms were more reserved, more alert; his head was up and looking from Linda to beyond her, as though he were reading her emotions and reacting to them. They shared a trust in each other. Zero relied on her and she relied on him. Despite her nerves revving up at the thought of running into a gunman, Linda kept her emotions as bottled up as possible. Zero absorbed her energy, both positive and negative. She wanted him alert but under control. Otherwise, his movements could give them away too soon. She glanced at Joe. The intensity with which he stared at the cabin added uncertainty to an otherwise intense situation. She couldn't predict what he'd do if he thought Aster was in imminent danger. His worry for his daughter had driven him this far, but he had to keep his self-control to provide his daughter the best chance possible.

They circled the cabin in silence, stopping behind the woodshed. Shadows of people moved behind the small frosted windows. The figures traveled at an even, unhurried pace. If only their identities were more visible. It would make her and Joe's next moves more obvious. She wasn't sure if they should rush the place, knock on the door, or hold back and wait for confirmation. Without additional information, waiting was the best option.

"I think I can sneak up to the window and look in." Joe motioned to the side window.

Linda shook her head. "Too much of a risk."

"I need to know if Aster's in there."

"I understand, but if they see you, it could compromise everyone."

"I need to know."

"Rushing close to the cabin without knowing what we're dealing with is not a good idea."

His expression tensed. "You don't get it. After losing Ivy, I refuse to lose Aster too. You have your whole family intact." He took a step toward the cabin.

Linda reached her arm out to stop him. "Don't tell me about loss. I carry the loss of my friends and colleagues with me every day. The memories of them in the best of times and at the moment they died haunt me over and over at night. But I also carry their hopes and their dreams." She spoke at a slow pace, holding him back with her words. "I have to continue living in the smartest way possible. If I rush into chaos without thinking through the possible effects of my actions, I bruise their memories. I was gifted this life. That means no jumping into superheroic actions that carry more risk than necessary. I want Aster and Payton safe. And I need you safe too. I also want whoever killed Noah to be brought to justice. Revealing ourselves too soon will place all of us at risk."

Chapter Eleven

Linda's plan made sense and stopped Joe from doing something stupid, like rushing to the cabin door. As of right now, she was the levelheaded one and he was becoming unhinged, his emotions threatening to override his good sense. He'd handled the bear with far more confidence than she had because he'd handled bears in the past. She'd handled police work for the military. Her understanding of tactics and best practices in dealing with this type of situation came from years of training and experience. His experience with something like this came from television shows and movies.

He stared at the cabin. The entire place was so silent, only branches in the wind made any sound. A mix of emotions washed over him. He wanted to find his daughter, but he also didn't want to complicate her situation. He closed his eyes and wished her back home, watching YouTube, propped up in her bed, texting her girlfriends and looking forward to Christmas Eve at the inn. The only consolation was that she was in the cabin and therefore warm. Despite all the hiking he and Linda had done, he never made it all the way to warm. His body had retained a chill all night, but he'd have been much colder if Linda hadn't made the fire.

Linda stood next to him, glancing around, Zero at her side. They were assessing the situation, and their calmness lowered Joe's irritation. He had to figure out a way to help his daughter without getting her killed in the process.

On the other side of the cabin, they saw the two snowmobiles, two-seaters with a lot of horsepower. The perfect way for them to travel back to his car, but if whoever was in the cabin turned out to be the bad guys, the machines could leave them behind. There was no way he and Linda could keep up with snowmobiles that went more than one hundred miles per hour.

He couldn't let that happen, so he waved over to Linda. "I have an idea. What if we prevent the snowmobiles from leaving?"

"We don't even know if Aster is in there. And don't you think it would be better if we could ride on them to get back rather than disable them?"

He thought about it. She was right, but something told him that the snowmobiles were the solution to their problems. "It will only be a temporary thing. I can reassemble them easy enough. I have a gut feeling about this."

She nodded, her expression breaking into a slight smile. "Then you should follow it. But please be careful. I don't want to have to rescue you too."

"But you would if I needed it?" Something warmed inside him at their easy camaraderie.

"Absolutely. What can I do to help?"

"Keep Zero back here and watch for anyone coming."

He crawled through the cover of trees toward the snowmobiles, which made him less visible, reduced the amount of footprints in the snow and took the pressure off his sore ankle. He'd been around snowmobiles all his life, fixing the used ones he picked up for a song when in his teens and playing with better versions as he made more money.

There was an eerie quiet around the cabin. Behind one iced-over window, there appeared to be a yellow-checkered curtain. If it were a furnishing in any other dwelling, it would have been charming. Puffs of gray smoke spiraled up and away from the chimney. When Joe had received his first snowmobile, a used Polaris INDY Sport, he couldn't afford to send the sled for yearly tune-ups or repairs. He'd taken apart nearly every piece of it and learned all he needed to know about it himself. He did the same with the four subsequent sleds he'd owned. He examined the twin Ski-Doo Grand Tourings in front of him, newer models with enough horsepower to climb the steep mountains around them. He carefully unhooked one of the wing covers over the engine. The ignition wiring sat right on top. He pulled it from the harness. His actions weren't meant to kill the machine; they were meant to slow an escape. With the right knowledge, it could be put back together in less than a minute.

Before he could pull the wiring in the other machine, the back door to the cabin opened. He dropped to the ground—silent, he hoped. Heavy footsteps thumped over the wooden porch and crunched on the snow. He tucked behind the snowmobile and held his breath, not moving a muscle. If he stuck his head out to get a better look, he would give himself away. If the person walked over to where he was hiding, Joe would be in a vulnerable spot. Either way, he was in trouble. He relied on Linda, watching from the trees, to help him if he needed it. The footsteps went off in the opposite direction, into the trees on the far side, away from them.

Linda froze as the man exited the house. Joe had hidden so quickly; she prayed he hadn't been seen. With her hand wrapped around Zero's chest, she could feel the low rumble coming from him, one breath short of a growl. The man headed to an outhouse about fifty yards from where she was crouched. The twentysomething-year-old was average height, dressed in a gray sweatshirt and jeans. There was no visible firearm on his person, but it could be under the sweatshirt. His eyes focused on the outhouse without a wayward glance in any other direction.

"Shh. It's okay. Shh." She reassured her dog that she had things under control. She was lying to him, but if he felt threatened for either of them, he might become overprotective. That would do more harm than good.

When the wooden door slammed shut, she released her tight hold on Zero. He was still next to her but able to shift in place. Joe appeared from behind the snowmobile, the tension visible in the lines on his face, the tautness of the muscles in his neck and his stiff posture. She leaned forward and motioned for him to get back down. He did.

The man came back a few minutes later, and only then did he glance around. He paused and stared past the trees surrounding Linda, then made an abrupt turn and went inside. For a few minutes, everything was silent except for the light wind rushing through the trees. Then Joe popped up next to her. She nearly jumped out of her shoes. Zero, on the other hand, wagged his tail and licked Joe in the face.

"I'm back."

Linda shook her head. "You scared me. When did you leave the snowmobiles?"

"When he was in the outhouse, I went the long way around. I only had time to handle one snowmobile, hopefully that'll be enough. Did you recognize the man?"

She wished she had. She'd be able to understand more of what they were up against. Instead, she shook her head. "Never saw him before."

"From the footprints around the snowmobile, there are only two men. Two smaller sets too. I'm sure the girls are here." He seemed primed to rush the cabin but was holding himself back. Barely. Linda couldn't blame him.

"So, four people. From what I've seen, it doesn't appear that Payton and Aster went willingly, but they might have. We need to be prepared for any possibility."

"There is no way Aster joined two men in the middle of the forest in a snowstorm without a really good reason." His voice began to rise, and she shushed him. They'd traveled too far to expose themselves.

"They left the house on foot and joined up with the snowmobiles later. They could have been trying to run from them."

"I am assuming these men are dangerous and my daughter is not an accomplice."

"I would agree. I need to understand all possibilities, though. I don't want to make a plan to rescue Payton and have her kicking and screaming as I drag her away. If we know what we're up against, we can plan accordingly. We need a better understanding of what's inside."

"How? The windows are all frosted."

"Zero and I can sneak up to the house and try to find a way to look inside."

"You're too short. I should do it."

"Okay. But be careful."

He looked back at her and nodded. "You too."

He slipped away again, and Linda prayed he wouldn't be noticed. He still mattered to her, and the fact he was hurting—not only from Aster's situation but also something else roiling through his unconscious—only made Linda want to help him more.

Joe hid behind a small propane tank. He limped all the way there but was able to stand on his weaker ankle. The night off it helped, but the inflammation could come roaring back.

The back door opened, and Payton, her eyes scanning the surrounding area outside the cabin, walked onto the porch, her fists clenched to her sides. Zero's energy shifted, and Linda rubbed her hand over his neck, keeping him steady until she could confirm what she was seeing. Payton made a jerky glance over her shoulder and into the cabin. When she reached the bottom stair, she sprinted toward the tree line. Two men now rushed out of the cabin. The man in the gray sweatshirt and another man—older, taller and dressed in jeans and a mid-length shearling coat—rushed outside after her.

"Stop!" the older man yelled waving a gun.

Payton kept her eyes in front of her as she ran. Within seconds, the man grabbed her and knocked her down. She landed with a thud, her head hitting the snow-covered ground.

Linda couldn't watch a teenage girl getting beaten up. "Chase," she commanded Zero.

He responded to Linda's attack command, rushing off at a high speed straight after the larger man with the gun. It was risky, but they were so isolated out here that Linda could think of no other way to stop him. Zero grabbed the man's gun-wielding arm. He shook his head back and forth until the man let Payton go to focus on the dog attack. She scrambled away from them.

Linda rushed forward. Instead of giving Zero a release command, she grabbed for the man's other arm. Struggling to break free, he swung widely. Zero wouldn't let him go; he had been trained to hold until she released him. She was thankful he obeyed.

A shot rang out. The gun was pointed at Linda, but Zero wrestled so much with the man's other arm, he twisted away just in time as the close-range bullet flew past him. Despite the loud noise, Zero held on to him. The man's free arm swung at Linda, striking her in the side of the head, knocking her to the cold ground.

Chapter Twelve

So much was happening, Joe had to focus on the most immediate danger, which was Linda. She and Zero had rushed to save Payton, putting their lives at risk. Payton had run off, followed by the younger man, and Aster was nowhere to be found. When the man with the gun struck Linda, Joe sprinted as fast as he could to her side, slamming into the man. Zero was still holding on to his arm, and Joe's force knocked Zero and the man to the ground.

The man used his foot to kick at Zero and tried to point his gun at Joe. Joe swiveled away from the barrel. He punched the man until he wrenched the gun away from him, then slung it as far away from him as possible. His entire being spun into survival mode. He held the man down, ready to knock him unconscious.

The door to the cabin opened, and Aster walked out. Joe froze. Even from the distance between them, he could see her face was bruised, her lip swollen. Before he could call out to her, the man slipped free of his heavy coat and Zero's jaws. Joe ran after him, but his ankle slowed him down.

Linda remained knocked out on the ground as Payton headed straight for the forest with someone else on her tail. Amid all the commotion, Aster paused, staring at her father. She wasn't wearing a coat or hat. That wouldn't be much of a problem in the streets of Birch Glen, but here in the middle of nowhere, where the winds blew stronger and the elevation welcomed colder temperatures, she could be knocked out by hypothermia before she walked a mile.

The large man Joe had just wrestled went after her. He had to be more than six foot four. Zero chased after him. When he jumped to grab him again, the man kicked him, sending him yelping and curled up against a tree.

Then the man was on Aster. She seemed so tiny next to this behemoth. She raced away toward the outhouse, a small wooden structure made of grayed wood and only a cut-out crescent-moon shape for a window. When Aster closed herself inside, Joe took several more silent steps toward them, then let loose, swinging at her captor. He punched his face, not moving him off balance at all; then he kicked at his legs. The man was a brick wall. His face twisted and he roared; his arm reached out and punched Joe off his feet and into the snow. Joe jumped up immediately and rushed him. The impact sent them both backward a few feet, two muscular and monstrous arms grasped Joe. As his feet left the ground, he realized he was outmatched.

The door to the outhouse swung open, and Aster cried out, "Dad!"

The man stared at Joe as though his name changed everything. That gave Joe a small opening. He swung his fists at the man's face. Blood flew out from his nose, but the man didn't release him. Aster rushed over to help and punched the man over and over, kicking him with all her might.

Without effort at all, he flung Joe into the side of a tree and grabbed Aster by the hair. Despite the wind being knocked out of him, Joe stood up again and chased the beast. Aster's screams drew Linda and Zero. The dog rushed over and clamped down on the man's arm. Again. Zero had been relentless despite the pain he was obviously suffering. The man released Aster and tried to fling the dog off him.

Joe ran to Aster and checked to see if she was okay. Despite tears from the pain of having her hair nearly yanked out, she was holding herself together.

"Are you okay?"

"Yes. I'm so sorry." Her words were caught between heavy breaths.

"Later. Stay here. Don't move."

When he turned back to Linda, she was fighting with the guy, Zero still holding on to his arm. The man fought off Linda while trying to shake Zero away. Blood seeped through his sweater. Zero was no longer holding back on his bite strength. The man swung back at Linda, and she shifted away with a speed that was amazing; then she ducked, pivoted and shot her leg out toward his stomach. This time, the man caught it, lifted her and flung her away, then pulled the scruff of Zero's neck and flung him off his arm. He sprinted away from them. Joe rushed toward him again, but the sound of an engine stopped him. The younger man had found Payton in the forest and dragged her to the snowmobile while they were fighting. The big guy ran toward them, jumped onto the back of the machine, holding Payton, and then they were leaving. Before they disappeared, the younger one pointed a gun toward the other snowmobile and shot the engine. Linda ran after them, but it was no use. They'd accelerated away without any chance of them catching up on foot.

"No!" Linda called out at the snow blown into the air by the snowmobile.

Although Joe had run off a bear earlier, he'd failed when it counted. The elation of rescuing Aster evaporated almost as soon as it arrived. There could be no celebration while Payton remained in danger.

Zero trotted toward them with a slight limp. His tail wagged as he approached Aster. She wrapped her arms around him and dropped her head into his fur. Joe crouched next to them, his hand resting on her shoulder.

"We'll get her back," he said.

She nodded but didn't look up. Zero remained at her side—no judgment, all love.

"Are you okay?" he asked again.

"I'm good." She wasn't the type to focus on her own needs when Payton was still in danger, but he didn't push. Instead, he turned to Linda.

"Are you okay?" they both said at once.

Joe shook his head. "I didn't imagine we'd fail. My

ankle is the same, and I may have bruised a rib when I hit the tree, but I'm ready to get us out of here. And you?"

"Embarrassed but physically fine. Hopefully, you can put the other snowmobile back together?"

"Maybe. I'd be more confident if they hadn't shot at the engine." He looked at the injured snowmobile he'd been so certain would keep the two men within their grasp. Instead, they'd taken off and left them with one that might be beyond repair.

Chapter Thirteen

Linda's body ached after getting struck in the head and then having her shoulder slam into the ground during her attempt at apprehending one of the men. The raging pain near her collarbone meant the year of physical therapy on her shoulder had just gone out the window. Not her best moment. Now they were stranded in the middle of the forest, and Payton was still in danger. She could handle situations where people were injured or even deceased, but this attack had hit close to her heart. She cared about Joe and, by extension, cared about Aster. And seeing Zero risk his life multiple times littered her mind with memories of the burning helicopter.

As Joe looked over the snowmobile, Linda needed to know Aster's state of mind after such a traumatic situation. The strain of the night before had cast shadows over the teen's eyes. Outside in only a sweatshirt, jeans and sneakers, she moved toward her father without obvious injury, although she should go to the hospital. She should have any physical injuries looked over, especially anything that wasn't obvious to the naked eye, and a mental health provider should speak to her as well. The trauma of the night would affect her to the core. Linda understood how trauma lingered, the nightmares that haunted her sleep required hours and hours of therapy, and the memories still affected her.

Joe had blood smeared across his face, perhaps from a broken nose. He didn't seem to notice; instead, he seemed focused on his daughter. He also had that sprained ankle to consider as they made their way out of the forest. Despite all that, he had run to his daughter and hugged her tightly. Aster rested her head on her father's shoulder. So many unsaid words, all put to the side with a hug and the love of a father for his child. There would be plenty of time to deal with the *who*, *what* and *why* of what had happened later, when they were all safe.

Linda then turned to Zero. After all they'd been through together, she hated the idea that he'd been injured again. Although it had been a full recovery, he was getting older and wasn't a superhero dog.

Zero shook out his fur and stepped close to her and kissed her face.

"How are you, boy?" She rubbed her fingers over his fur, feeling for any sore spots or other signs of injury. After finding nothing, she let out a sigh of relief. "We have a bit more work to do. Are you up to it?"

He barked and wagged his tail.

First things first: find the firearm.

It had been Joe who wrestled the gun away from one of the men. She searched the area and found it covered in snow. An M1911, a military-grade semiautomatic, using a .45 ACP round. She took a deep breath. Had that size bullet hit Zero point-blank, he wouldn't have stood a chance. The magazine could hold seven rounds; it had five bullets left, including one in the chamber. This gun could have been the one to shoot Noah. She put the safety on and placed it in the side pocket of her pack for easy access. She handled it with her gloves on but wasn't going to worry too much about fingerprint preservation if they came back and started shooting. She needed a weapon, and this one would do just fine.

With the firearm out of the way, she lifted the long coat Zero had pulled off their attacker—a large shearling coat with definite bite marks in one of the arms. She checked the pockets. There was a receipt in one to the local hardware store. She could hand that to her father to follow up.

She turned back to the snowmobile. The bullet hole went straight into the engine. Not that she could see behind the black fiberglass cover, but it looked bad. She followed Joe over to examine it, but she'd never been too good with engines and mechanical things.

As he pulled open the side panel that gave access to the engine, she went to Aster, who was standing with her arms crossed, her expression raw. Linda had seen that look before on victims of violent crime: doubt that anything could go back to normal after this.

"How are you feeling?" Linda asked her.

She shrugged. "Okay."

"'Okay' as in, 'My physical body is fine, but I'm freaked out by what happened' or, 'I have a few bruises and I'm terrified'?"

"I have a few bruises from when Jeff pushed me into a table, but otherwise, they left Payton and me alone. They were too focused on getting back the stuff someone stole from them." Her face showed the strain of the evening but nothing shattering to a young woman's psyche. That was good. Still, Linda would want her to speak to a trauma counselor once they got back. She'd talk to Joe about it when they had a less intense moment.

"Who is Jeff?" she asked in as easy a tone as she could muster under the circumstances. "Which one was that?"

"He was Noah's friend. The one in the gray sweatshirt."

"Noah's friend?" And now Noah was dead. The image of a young life gone too early stuck in Linda's head. No matter how long she had worked in the military, certain things hit her to the core. She'd stop being human if they didn't.

"Noah was going to call the police. He was really mad Jeff had been using his house without his permission."

"Did you catch the name of the older man?"

"Roman, I think? Noah called him that. He has an accent." She stared at the coat in Linda's arms.

"From where?"

Aster pursed her lips. "I don't know. German or something like that."

"Are you cold?"

She shrugged, despite having her arms wrapped around herself and being able to see her breath. Her face had lost color except for redness on her nose. The thinness of her sweatshirt and her lack of gloves would cause frostbite on a long snowmobile drive.

"Where's your coat?" Linda asked her.

"I left it in Payton's car back at the house." She stood up straighter, as though the cold had no effect on her, but the temperature couldn't be more than twenty degrees, and a sweatshirt would not be adequate.

Linda took off her dark blue shell and down parka and handed them to her. "Take this. It's too cold to travel without a coat, and these are very warm together. They should protect you against the wind as we drive."

"I couldn't do that," she said, refusing the offer.

"Let me give her my jacket. You need to stay warm as well," Joe argued with her. He began stripping off his own coat.

Linda shook her head. "This makes the most sense. I can wear this." She held up Roman's coat. "It's warm and I don't mind carrying it with us in case someone can identify him wearing it in Birch Glen or the surrounding areas. Besides, Aster will be closer to the front with you. She needs something warmer to wear. Trust me. I'll have Zero to help block the wind." Not that she feared being cold in such a thick coat.

She also gave Aster her gloves and knit hat. That hat had been thick enough where it was folded over to protect her head from the worst of the man's strikes. "Here, take this. I'll be fine for a bit."

Aster pulled a red mitten out of her back pocket. "Thank you. I lost one of my gloves on the snowmobile. They wouldn't turn around to get it."

"You're in luck. Your dad found it."

Joe turned around and tossed Aster the mitten. There was a hint of a smile on Aster's face when she caught it. "Thanks, Dad. Did you know it was mine?"

"Of course I did. I gave them to you last Christmas. They're one of a kind, like you."

Aster nodded, hugging the glove to her.

When she was all bundled up, Linda pushed her a bit more. "Can you tell me how you ended up here?"

"Natie wanted a ride home from the party. When we got there, we ran into Noah first. He said some guy named Jeff wanted to speak with Payton. We went into the kitchen for a drink, and that's when we heard someone ripping apart the room upstairs. Noah screamed at them to leave. Payton panicked, and we ran into the backyard. Noah ran from the house behind us because Roman had a gun pointed at him. That's when we saw Roman shoot Noah. We ran as far as we could. Roman and Jeff found us, and by then we were so cold, we didn't fight them when they offered to take us back to the house. Stupid mistake. They took us here instead."

"Not stupid. He'd already killed one person. If you'd fought him, he might have killed you too. You did the best you could under the circumstances."

Regret clouded Aster's expression. It was easy to second-guess all the decisions made in the heat of a situation, but the past was unalterable. They had to deal with the present if they wanted to get out of here and help Payton.

"Looks like the gunshot dented the exhaust manifold." Joe had the snowmobile hood up, his bare hands covered in grease. "Give me a few minutes to start it up. This shouldn't affect the performance."

That was a huge relief. Linda had not been enthusiastic about hiking out of there with Joe needing to rely on a bad ankle.

As she waited for him, she went into the cabin. Zero followed her.

The inside was tidy and practical. Everything appeared only a few years old, as though whoever owned the cabin had retrofitted it for modern comforts but kept the rustic exterior. A bunk bed in the back corner; a woodstove in the middle of the room; an industrial sink with a hand pump, which meant someone had had the foresight and money to drill a well into the ground. The propane tank outside was attached to a small generator.

Zero's body language changed when he walked past the woodstove. His nose went to the floor.

"What have you found, Zero?" She didn't give him the search command because it was strictly used for narcotics. He only alerted to certain drugs. He continued to sniff until he reached the corner of the cabin. The corner seemed empty except for a broom and tongs and a poker for the fire. Despite the lack of anything, he turned to her and sat. Sitting was his alert that he'd located something.

"What is it?" She looked around and didn't see anything.

Zero stayed in place, adding a muffled bark. Something was there. She looked at a wall made of solid wood logs. Nothing. She got on her hands and knees and inspected the floor. It all seemed solid. He wasn't perfect—no dog was—but this alert was too certain. She knocked on the floorboards. One sounded more hollow than the others. She went over to the kitchen area and found a kitchen knife in a drawer and wedged it between the floorboards. The hollow one lifted. The nails in it weren't attached to anything.

Inside the hidden hole lay several pills in a clear sandwich bag. She lifted the bag from the hole, then examined one of the pressed pills. OxyContin, from its appearance, but fentanyl often appeared in counterfeit ones with deadly results. She'd seen these drugs brought onto her military base. The effects devastated families. Her father had mentioned that drug dealers had become more aggressive in Vermont over the past few years, resulting in several overdoses. Perhaps these two men were the pipeline into the community. Her mind raced over all the possibilities, but the scenario made a lot of sense. Smaller dealers dealt with bigger and bigger dealers who worked for large cartels.

She rifled through the cabinets, locating some canned goods and liquor. Not much. She also found a bag of unopened nuts. She checked the expiration date. They were still good, and she was starving. Joe and Aster would be too. She also refilled her water containers with the pumped water.

When she was done, she headed back outside to see if Joe had found a way to salvage the snowmobile. He was manipulating a few of the wires. He hopped on the seat and, after a few false starts, got the machine running. The roar of the engine was the sweetest music she could hear.

"Hot-wiring snowmobiles?" she asked.

"It's a skill set I don't regret having. I fixed a lot of motors after high school at Michael's Autoworks. Snowmobiles, ATVs, motorcycles. I never used it to steal anything, but it came in handy when people lost their keys or had an emergency. Scout's honor." He raised his hand and did the three-finger sign scouts all over the world used.

"I believe you. Besides I consider this an emergency." She waved Zero over. "We better go."

Chapter Fourteen

⸎

They had only an eighth of a tank of gas. Joe had no way of knowing how far they were traveling, but time was of the essence if they wanted to catch up to help Payton. He pulled out his phone and glanced at the map. The GPS marked their current location, provided a sense of direction and also showed a few landmarks in the vicinity. He hopped in the driver's seat; Aster sat behind him in the middle. There was limited room left on the sled, so Linda handed Joe her backpack. He nodded, putting it on backward so it covered his chest, allowing more room for passengers. Then she called Zero to her side. Aster shifted forward so Linda could squeeze him in between them. Zero hesitated but then hopped up on her lap. Linda maneuvered him sideways to fit and held on to his harness with one hand and wrapped her other arm in front of his chest to keep him from jumping off. She nodded toward Joe when she was ready.

It wasn't comfortable, but they could all get out. There should be more than enough horsepower to carry everyone up the mountain. Joe had to take a few breaths to calm his mind. His daughter was safe behind him, but Payton was still at risk. He wanted to rejoice, but how could he when another girl the same age as Aster was still missing? He reached behind and squeezed his daughter's arm, relieved she was safe and by his side. Then he punched the gas and left the cabin behind them.

Following the freshly made snowmobile tracks, he swerved around trees and over frozen brooks. This was a far cry from hiking through the forest in the middle of a snowstorm and much easier on his sore ankle. He made good time but couldn't speed because they weren't as secure with three people and a dog on the sled. A lack of helmets also had him driving in a more controlled manner. He had so much precious cargo on board. Aster, his heart; and Linda, who had placed herself at risk to help him and his family. His heart held a place for her too. She looked out for people in everything she did, not in a baked-apple-pie or clean-the-house kind of way, the warm way Ivy had shown her love. Instead, Linda stepped into danger to protect others. Had she not been with him, he would never have found Aster as quickly as they did. Yet in the process, she'd injured herself. And she not once complained. For the first time since Ivy had died, he had faith that things could get better.

The cold air whipped across his face. He didn't have glasses to block the wind, and his gloves weren't adequate on a snowmobile. At least there were hand warmers built into the handlebars to ease the sting.

As he followed the VAST trail, he searched for cut-offs that would lead to the Primley place. Aster tapped his shoulder and pointed ahead of them. Sure enough, fresh tracks sped into the woods up ahead. They were headed in the right direction. He gave her a thumbs-up and followed, hoping it wouldn't lead to an ambush. It wasn't possible to conceal the approach of a gas engine this size.

He slowed down as he made out the outline of the huge ski chalet behind the trees. "This is as far as I feel comfortable taking us," he said, shutting down the engine.

Linda let Zero go. The dog hopped off the seat and shook out his fur. Linda hopped off as well and reattached Zero's leash. Aster slid off the seat to follow.

Joe paused when he looked at Aster. He couldn't risk her getting caught up in this again. "I need you to remain here until we come back and get you."

"I'm not a child. I've handled myself fine so far."

"Witnessing a murder and getting taken hostage are not even close to handling anything." He didn't want to yell at her, but he also wanted her to understand how scared he was for her safety. Staying hidden would allow him to focus on getting Payton back. "Just stay here. I won't be able to think straight if I'm worrying about you."

She frowned but got back on the snowmobile and remained there.

He walked over to her and gave her a hug. Kissing the top of her head, he took a deep breath. Yes, he'd been mad at her for leaving without permission, but now that she was back, he was thankful she was alive and well and at his side. "I love you, buddy," he said, referring to her with the nickname he'd used since she was barely able to stand.

"Love you, too, Dad." She sat down, tears in her eyes.

Linda walked over to her and gave her a handful of nuts.

"Where are those from?" Joe asked as she gave him a handful too.

"Enemy territory." She ate a few. "They hit the spot. I was getting weak with hunger."

He followed Linda through the branches of the trees. The other sled was parked at the back door. The area where Noah had been killed had been marked off with police tape. His body was still there, the snow still stained in blood. The area appeared even stranger without any police presence at all. Someone would have remained at the scene, wouldn't they?

And why had Roman and Jeff returned to the scene of the crime? It made no sense. Joe would have thought they'd hightail it out of there. Unless what they were looking for was worth such a huge risk.

They moved toward the front of the house. An Expedition with Birch Glen Police on the side was pulled up near the entry stairs. Relief flooded Joe, but a creepy feeling mingled with the relief. He welcomed the support, especially having to handle so much on a bad ankle and with his daughter so close to the violence. A glance at Linda, however, crumbled his newly restored optimism. She'd placed her ungloved hand on the hood of the SUV and mouthed, "Cold," to him. The SUV had been here awhile, and so far there was no sign of anyone, not even Roman and Jeff. Linda tried to open the door of the police car, but it was locked.

"This doesn't feel right," Linda whispered. "Can I have the pack?"

He nodded and handed it to her. Before securing it to her back, she pulled out a gun from the side pocket.

"Have you always had that?"

She shook her head. "It's the one from Roman. I thought we might need it." She slipped it into the large pocket in the brown coat she was wearing. Easy access. "I hope I never have to use it, but since these men already killed one person and we have a police officer missing, I'm taking no chances. But we need to be extra safe. If there's a police officer here, that's one more person who is armed. I don't want to be mistaken for someone I'm not."

They went around the house to the back door. The door was locked, but the window next to it had been opened an inch, perhaps to get fresh air in the basement during the party the night before. A gas can had been knocked over, a puddle of gas soaking into the doormat. He picked it up and set it in the snow, away from the house.

"Be careful. The gas is all over this mat," he said as he tried the door.

"Thanks for the warning." She moved away from the door. "Zero and I will wait over here."

Joe pulled the window open and slipped through, less hampered than Linda by the backpack and the dog. Once inside, he heard shuffling off in the distance. Without spending too much time trying to understand the sounds he was hearing, he made his way to the back door and opened it for her.

Once both were inside, they stood in silence, listening for anything. Sounds came from the opposite end of the house. Voices, footsteps, rustling. Linda carried the gun in her hand, her finger resting over the trigger, not in it. She held Zero's leash in her other hand. They trod softly across the wooden floor into the kitchen. Zero remained close at her side. He had enough leash to move forward but not too far away from her.

The house appeared different in the daylight: massive windows overlooking the mountains brightened everything from the pine kitchen cabinets to the gray stone of the fireplace. Too much light. There was no place to hide in such open spaces, except maybe the island in the middle of the room.

The sound of breaking glass and yelling came from upstairs. It sounded like Roman and Jeff. No one else was heard. That did not bode well for the presence of a police officer. The only consolation was that the noise might have masked the approach of their snowmobile, which would give Joe and Linda the element of surprise.

To get out of the main area, Linda waved him into a small kitchen pantry. They could remain close to the sounds without being seen. The tension had them all on high alert. Linda let out a heavy breath as her hand reached down to ease Zero. Joe clenched his fist, wanting a weapon and hoping they wouldn't need to use one.

"He told me he lost it." The voice was that of a younger man, perhaps Jeff. He was upstairs, down the hall. Aster had explained to Linda that she'd heard the men arguing upstairs when she was in the kitchen the night before. She and Payton had stood in the kitchen, rushed outside at the arguing, only to watch a man be killed only a few minutes later. Joe couldn't imagine her going through something like that and maintaining enough sense to realize they needed to escape.

Something smashed against a wall or on the floor. "No one loses that amount of anything. He's lying to you." This man spoke with a Russian accent.

"It's not here."

"Then we go there. He can choose—her or the money."

They remained still as the footsteps up the stairs moved farther away from them.

"You should wait here. Zero won't be silent moving up the stairs," Joe said, pointing to the uncarpeted stairs.

She frowned. "How's your ankle?"

"Fine," he said, exaggerating the truth.

She lifted a brow, then nudged him with her elbow, a softness for him reflected in her eyes, but her focus remained clear. "Go ahead, but be careful."

The faith she had in him motivated him to both complete the task and make sure he made it out alive, not only for her but for his daughter, who waited patiently outside for him. He moved in as much silence as he could up the stairs, but the wood creaked and his heart beat through his chest. He ignored the pain in his ankle, trying not to think about the damage he continued to inflict on it. He'd rest and recover when this nightmare was over.

When he turned the corner, he froze. In the center

of the hallway, Dylan lay back against the wall. A single shot to the head left his blood splattered across the whole area. The image seared itself into Joe's brain. He'd never unsee his friend's dead body. Dylan had supported Joe's dreams and helped him after Ivy's death. He'd even babysat Aster when Joe had no other options.

He knelt beside him, trying to think of something he could do to change the outcome. He bowed his head in prayer, in memoriam, in regret, but Linda, who must have followed him, pulled him back. "We don't have time. Focus on Payton."

The argument down the hall brought him into the present. He stepped away from Dylan.

"Leave her here. She's useless." Jeff sounded more panicked than demanding. It wasn't a good sign. Tensions were running high, and both men might be armed and dangerous.

"That's not how this works. She's the leverage we need. It was a mistake ever trusting you in this."

Joe heard something strike a wall. Then it sounded like a body fell to the ground. He wanted to move closer but was unarmed and afraid he'd only cause Payton to be harmed.

Roman appeared in the hallway, dragging Payton by the arm. She fought him every step. She swung her arm toward his face, but he caught it and held both her arms close to her body and continued down the hall, dodging her kicks.

Joe dove at Roman, wrapping an arm across his neck and knocking him to the ground, sending Payton flying away from them. She landed on the floor and hustled away. Roman punched at Joe's head, but Joe shifted in time to avoid the brunt of the force, merely getting grazed by the back of his knuckles. He twisted and punched his elbow into Roman's chest, ejecting the air from the man's lungs. He then grabbed Roman by the collar and pulled him back to his feet.

"You're not going anywhere." His arms shook as he pressed Roman into the wall.

Roman relaxed for a moment, then, without any warning, headbutted Joe, sending him onto the ground. The pain drowned out Joe's senses. When he wrestled himself back, Roman ran past the bottom stair and rushed out the front door. Joe shook off the collision and tried to stand up. Roman had already escaped. He went over to Payton. "Are you okay?"

Her face had a scratch on it, and she was barely able to stand up, Joe wasn't sure whether she was physically injured or emotionally shut down. He placed an arm around her. "It's going to be all right."

Linda stood behind them. "Wait here. I've got this." She released Zero to run after Roman and raced after him down the stairs.

Payton watched them rush away and asked Joe, "Do you have Aster?"

"She's fine. Waiting outside." He helped her to the family room and told her to remain hidden behind the bar until someone came for her. He had no idea if Roman would circle back, because he seemed to want Payton as collateral of some sort.

Zero barked outside in the distance, and Joe prayed Linda would be okay.

Chapter Fifteen

Zero chased Roman through the front door. Linda hoped
her dog would be able to stop him without getting hurt—
or worse, killed in the process. It was a fear she carried
with her constantly. It was the price of having a canine
working in such dangerous situations. Zero ran down
the porch. Linda trotted behind, watching for anyone
coming up on her left or right side as she raced into the
front yard. She held the gun, ready to shoot if required.

As Roman had lost his sidekick and his hostage,
Linda prepared for any desperate action taken by a person whose plan was falling apart. He climbed inside
Joe's Jeep, opening the back door from the front seat.
Zero jumped inside. As soon as he was inside, Roman
fled the front seat and slammed the back door to close
Zero inside. Zero barked and scratched frantically at
the door. Now it was only Linda and Roman. He raced
toward the back of the house where the snowmobile
was parked. She was too far away to get a good shot.
Instead, she sprinted after him. He swerved away from

the snowmobile by the back door, pushing through the bushes toward Aster's location. Linda tried to cut him off. But it was too late. Within seconds, he had his arm around Aster's neck and a gun pointed to her temple.

Linda aimed her weapon at him. "I can't let you leave here with her."

Aster struggled until Roman struck the grip of the gun over her ear. She cried out in pain as her fight fizzled out.

Roman called back to Linda. "You can't stop me. Did you really think she'd be safe out here alone? I saw your arrival out the window. Leaving her isolated made her the perfect backup plan. And here we are."

She pointed the gun at him. He was right: she couldn't be sure she wouldn't hit Aster if she took a shot. All he had to do was shift an inch, and Aster could die by Linda's bullet. She froze, terror caught in her throat, yet she continued to aim the gun.

"I'm not leaving town until I have what's mine. We can make this easy or far more bloody. It's up to you."

"What do you want? I can help get it for you—just let her go. She's got nothing to do with this and will only increase the number of people wanting you behind bars."

"First, I want my coat back." He pointed the gun toward Linda.

"Send her over here and it's yours."

"Not a chance."

"Then you'll freeze." She wouldn't back down, because as soon as he had the coat, he could hurt Aster.

"I don't think so. I can handle cold weather. Let's see if she can." The menace in his voice had nothing to do with the gun in his hand and everything to do with a complete disregard for Aster's life. Linda had been to hostage-situation training, but she was by no means an expert in the field.

She needed to understand what he wanted. Someone had stolen from him, and he wanted whatever it was back or he'd make them pay. She took a chance… "Can Jeff help you?"

"Not in his condition." He had a smirk on his face.

"Did you kill him?" she asked.

"I didn't wait to take his pulse. Why don't you check on him? The girl and I have somewhere to be."

"If you hand over Aster, I'll go anywhere with you."

"No, thanks. I already had a punch to the jaw because of you. This one isn't as well trained."

"I won't let you get away from here with her, but I'll go willingly."

He pointed the gun toward her, and she swallowed hard and remained as composed as possible. She'd seen football-player-size marines drop to their knees and beg for their lives with a gun pointed at their heart, but begging wasn't her style. Surviving was.

She could hear a car arriving in the front of the house. Backup for her or a getaway car for Roman? She prayed it was backup. Footsteps came from behind her, and a shot rang out from Roman's gun. She turned to see Joe flat on the ground.

"Dad!" Aster screamed.

Roman remained, with the gun pointed away from her and waving between Linda and Joe. Aster struggled to get away, but he gripped her tightly, his hand clutching her neck, causing her to gasp for breath. "She might be more cooperative unconscious."

Joe lifted his head. His whole body froze when he saw Aster in Roman's grip. "Stop. Leave her here."

"One step forward, and your daughter is dead." He stared down at Aster. The composure she'd held together for so long deteriorated, and through sobs and useless thrashing, Aster swayed on her feet, held up by his hand on her neck.

"Don't harm her. Do what you want with me, but please, let her go," Joe said.

"Touching, but she's easier to carry."

Linda glanced back and saw two police officers coming up behind them, guns drawn.

"Freeze. Drop your weapon," one of them called out. It was Officer Maura Gates.

"Sorry, sweetheart, we already had this discussion. It's time for me to go."

He backed up with Aster between him and the three guns pointed in their direction. Linda switched her aim to the snowmobile to take it out and stop his getaway, but Joe made a surprise rush attack, perhaps hoping to get Roman to take his arm off Aster and give her a chance to escape.

A flash of light blinded her for a moment. The entire side of the house was ablaze. Payton was still inside—so were Jeff and the remains of Officer Dylan Graham.

By the time she'd regained her bearings, Roman had Aster on the snowmobile he'd arrived on. When the engine roared alive, Joe rushed toward them, and Linda followed, but they were too late. The snowmobile sped off into the trees, snow billowing behind them. Aster's cries faded away as the machine traveled into the forest.

Joe rushed after them on foot, the injury to his ankle evident in his weakened strides. Before the sound of the engine disappeared into the mountain, he turned to the other snowmobile. His hands shook as he struggled to open the hood and start the engine. Linda stepped closer to assist him, but he waved her off.

"I'll be faster alone," he said.

She nodded.

When the engine started up, he revved the gas and raced away. She glanced down at the gun in her hand. She should have given it to Joe, but it was too late. He was long gone.

Officer Gates and Officer Ryan Faruk came up to her. She hadn't noticed their presence until Officer Gates placed her hand on Linda's shoulder.

"Are you hurt?" she asked.

Linda shook her head. "I'm good, but there are people in the house." She turned away from the fiery back door and rushed toward the front entrance. She slid the gun into her pocket.

Icy wind couldn't ease Joe's distress. After seeing the body count rise around him, he struggled to keep his focus as he drove after Roman. The distress in Aster's eyes and the sound of her calling out to him punched straight into the center of his heart. He'd been let down by prayer in the past, but in the middle of the biggest storm of his life, he couldn't carry on without help. *Please, God, make sure Aster is safe.*

The engine sputtered and slowed down to a stop. The gas gauge had dropped to zero. "You have got to be kidding me." He dropped his head onto the handles, and he let out a loud roar. The other snowmobile was far enough away that he could only hear the faintest hum off in the distance. His best bet would be to hike back to where he'd come from while it was still light out. He wouldn't survive another night in the cold, not without Linda and her supplies.

As he limped back over the trail, his anger at Linda grew. He'd trusted that she and Zero would stop Roman, not enable him to take his daughter. Zero had ended up locked in his car, and she'd pointed her weapon at Roman but refused to take him out. Maybe he'd been wrong about her. She wasn't brave at all. She'd waited for him to arrive before attempting to stop Roman from escaping. She could have shot at the snowmobile; she could have taken out his leg. Zero could have chased him down before Roman dragged away Aster. So many options, and instead, Aster was lost to him. Linda thought he needed more faith. He needed a tank of gas, a better ankle and his daughter in his arms.

I can't believe you let me down again.

Chapter Sixteen

The trauma of seeing so many dead and injured at the helicopter crash a year before had warped her reaction to the current situation. She had to focus on getting whoever was inside to safety. She rushed around the building and through the front door, following Officer Faruk. Officer Gates remained outside on her radio. Linda left Zero in the safety of Joe's Jeep as she focused on getting Payton and the others out before fire overwhelmed the building. Once inside, Officer Faruk ran up the stairs, pausing where Dylan had been shot.

"Payton?" Linda called out on the main floor. She rushed about the room, glancing over furniture and into any other areas. She found Payton hiding behind the bar. The confident high school senior had transformed into someone unsure of everything.

"We need to get out of here. The house is on fire." Linda signaled her to come out.

"Mr. Webster told me to stay hidden."

Linda clasped her by the arms and helped her stand.

"He was right to tell you to stay inside, but the situation has changed."

Payton's face was pale, but she was breathing and able to walk out on her own. She'd be okay. They went to the front door. Officer Gates met them and helped Payton to her police car. When Linda was certain Payton was in a good place, she went back toward the house, ignoring Zero's frantic barking. He would want to follow her, but she knew where her next target was.

Before she went back inside, she paused, holding the door for Officer Faruk, who was carrying Dylan's body in his arms. Linda's heart ached as she watched him lay his colleague in the snow to try to save his life. It was no use. His life was already gone.

She was glad someone had recovered his body. Several of her own team had been lost in the helicopter crash, their bodies nearly unrecognizable by the time they'd been pulled from the flames. Dylan's family could avoid such a horrible fate. She shifted her focus to Jeff—one of the reasons Dylan had lost his life. There was so much anger inside her, but she had a job to do, and if Jeff was still alive, he deserved a chance. He'd been upstairs in the back bedroom away from the kitchen. She should have enough time to get him out before the entire house was consumed by the flames, but fires had a way of creeping through a house unseen, through venting and between floors. She respected that the fire was far more powerful than she was.

From the way Roman described knocking Jeff to the ground, Linda expected him to be unconscious or worse. It didn't matter. She had to find him. As she ran up the stairs, fire leaped down from a wall onto a curtain and ignited an upholstered chair. The idea of being trapped inside this growing inferno sent shivers through her, but she remained focused on her goal. After all, it had been her job to help people. This urge to pitch in during an emergency would never leave her. It was as much a part of her as her optimism.

The foul smell of burning plastic and material tainted the air. The intense heat coming from the kitchen mocked her after her night complaining about the cold. Two more stairs, and she made it to the top landing. She hustled to the room she'd seen Roman drag Payton out of. A haze of smoke made her line of vision murky, but after a few steps inside, she saw Jeff.

He was lying on the bedroom floor, unconscious. His arm was twisted into an uncomfortable break. Perhaps the work of Roman. Luckily, the fire hadn't spread this far yet. She knelt by him, prepared for a fight in case he came to and was confused. She checked his pulse and breathing. He was bleeding from the head, but his vital signs indicated he was still alive.

"Jeff, wake up." She shook his shoulders. He didn't budge, but his chest rose and fell. He wouldn't be alive for long if she left him here. "Jeff, wake up." She shook him again.

This time he groaned. Good. She shifted to position her better arm around him to pull him to his feet. Lifting him was difficult without any help from him; he acted as a dead weight. She'd only be able to get him out with a fireman's carry. Not an easy task with her bad shoulder, but she didn't have a choice. Any broken bones he had or a spinal cord injury would have to be dealt with later. If he remained here, he'd die. As her CO had always said, "You can fix a lot of things, but you can't fix dead."

Sirens screamed in the background. The firefighters must have arrived, but she couldn't wait for them as they cleared room by room.

She squatted and lifted Jeff to a near-standing position. His almost two hundred pounds slumped toward the floor. She shifted her legs as she struggled to hold him up, then grabbed his hand and moved his entire torso over her shoulders. She let out a sharp exhale and marched toward the bedroom door. She looked over the balcony and saw Officer Faruk by the front entrance.

He was waving her back. "The fire is under the stairs. Stay off them."

She stared at the wall of flames creeping toward them from the kitchen area. *You have got to be kidding.* She was not going to leave Jeff behind, but she wouldn't risk both of them by scrambling into a death trap.

"Okay, Jeff, we're going to try a different exit." She scanned the bedroom, which had been trashed during the earlier argument. There was no other exit, only a closet, bed, reading chair, television and two large windows looking out over the mountains. "Through the window, it is. Relax. I've got this," she said, more to assure herself than Jeff.

Smoke had started to eat up the fresh air and made remaining inside difficult. She wasn't a firefighter and didn't have the equipment to continue in this environment much longer. Her shoulder ached, reminding her of all the limitations she couldn't ignore.

To open the window, she rolled him onto his back on the bed. He moaned, which continued to be a good sign, but he didn't wake. She rushed back to the bedroom door and slammed it shut to slow the spread of the fire. She then opened one of the windows and yelled out, trying to catch the attention of anyone. The window was on the side of the house away from where the police and firetrucks had converged. She grabbed a yellow sweatshirt from the floor and waved it with all her might. If no one saw it, she'd be forced to drop Jeff out the second floor to the snow below. Normally, that wouldn't be so dangerous, but the house was on a hill, and the drop from the second floor was more like three floors with the incline. The fall could kill him, but if they remained inside, they'd both die. At least he stood a better chance in the snow. She said a quick thank-you for the snowfall the night before. The depth might be enough for an almost-safe landing. It had to be.

"One more time, Jeff," she said, lifting him up and transporting him to the window. A shiver rocked through her. She ignored it. The military hadn't trained her how to drop a living person out a window in a way that had the best chance of survival.

"Linda?" someone called up to her. It was Tom Hollis, a firefighter she'd gone to high school with. "Need some help?"

"Yes, please!"

"Hang tight." He disappeared around the corner.

Jeff shifted on her shoulders, his weight unbalancing Linda. She nearly dropped backward with him but found the windowsill in time to keep herself upright.

"Hold on, Jeff. A few minutes more." She swayed back and forth, adjusting his weight and calming her own nerves.

Four firefighters and Officer Gates rushed around the building and looked up. One of them slipped on the snowy incline and scrambled to get to his feet.

"What do you want me to do? Do you have an inflatable cushion?" Linda asked.

Tom yelled up to her, "No. Can you drop him into the snow? We'll be here to pull him out of the way for you."

As he spoke, everyone pushed as much snow as they could directly under the window, creating a better landing site. Not as good as a collapsible air mattress, but it was something.

"I'll try." She moved as close to the window as she could.

Everyone stood back, waiting for her to drop Jeff. She just had to make sure his limbs wouldn't get stuck in the window. If they did, he could land wrong and break his neck.

"On the count of three." Tom pointed to the snow pile.

"Okay," she called back.

"One. Two. *Three*."

She forced as much of her body out the window as possible to allow Jeff the best chance possible of not getting hurt further. He twisted as he fell but somehow landed on his back in the middle of the soft mound of snow.

There was no fanfare for her accomplishment. An ambulance team rushed toward him and placed him on a stretcher. Several members shoveled more snow under the window, this time for her.

"Try to land like you're sitting on a trampoline, okay?"

"Okay." She saw the snow. It was deep, but if she landed wrong... No. She wouldn't think about it.

"At the count of three."

She gave a thumbs-up.

"One. Two. *Three.*"

She leaped out the window, the rush of cold air a blessing. The ground came up fast. When she hit, snow billowed around her, packing into her sleeves and up her pant legs. The chill woke her up from the daze of saving Jeff and provided a sense of relief. After she safely landed, the team brought in another stretcher. She waved it away.

"I'm fine."

Officer Gates shook her head. "You need oxygen."

"I need to make sure Zero is okay, and Aster, and Joe." Everyone she cared about. She stood up and wobbled a bit. Officer Gates put her arm around Linda's waist and assisted her to an ambulance. The engine was running, and warmth flowed out the open door, where Payton was sitting on one of two stretchers inside the ambulance. An oxygen mask covered her face, but otherwise she appeared in good shape.

"How are you feeling?" Linda asked.

"Okay, thanks to you. I don't think I inhaled much smoke, but they want me to have oxygen just in case." A tear fell down her cheek. Then her head dropped into her hands and she sobbed. A normal reaction for a terrible twenty-four hours.

One of the EMTs had followed them over. "Hi, Linda.

I'm Alexa. I need to do a quick exam and give you some oxygen. It's protocol. Would that be okay?"

Before Linda could respond, the ambulance swirled around her, causing her to lose her balance. Several hands caught her and guided her to a stretcher.

Chapter Seventeen

Joe heard the commotion at the Primley place before he saw it. As he came closer, he could make out police lights and a blaze at the house. He picked up speed despite the pain in his ankle, his exhaustion and the chill gnawing on every bone in his body.

He looked around for Linda in the crush of people but couldn't find her. Had she gone into the fire? He rushed over to the police car. Officer Ryan Faruk was there, a regular at the inn's restaurant with his wife each Friday. Next to him was a body lying in the snow, covered with a tarp.

"Who?" Joe demanded.

"Dylan." Ryan swallowed hard and stepped toward Joe, leaving his friend and colleague behind him. "Any update on Roman? Linda filled us in on what happened at the cabin."

"No. All I know is, Aster was taken. I don't know where they went except through the forest on the trails."

Ryan nodded. "We have an APB out for them and

have units from the neighboring towns staking out the main snowmobile-parking areas. We would have been up here earlier but couldn't get through the snow. Only Dylan could make the climb with the chains on his tires." He glanced toward the fallen officer and shook his head.

Joe nodded. There was so much going on around them, but as long as Aster was missing, he had only one focus. He clenched his fists at his sides. He couldn't lose Aster.

"We're doing everything we can," Ryan said. "Hang in there."

"You know that's impossible."

An explosion smashed through the family room window of the house, flames wrapping around the window frames and reaching toward the roof. Ryan leaped backward, and Joe nearly fell to the ground. The entire world seemed to be falling apart.

"Where's Linda?" Joe asked.

"She's fine. Once a marine, always a marine." As a former marine himself, Ryan had a soft spot for Linda.

"What do you mean?"

"She rescued Payton and Jeff from the burning house. That woman is made of steel."

Joe stared at the house. Half the house was burning. "Where is she?"

Ryan pointed to the closest ambulance. "She needed oxygen after inhaling smoke, but that's standard care."

Joe walked over toward the two ambulances as another fire truck arrived. Each step toward Linda seemed a million miles farther from Aster, but there was no path toward her. The police wouldn't speak to him besides a trite "We're on this. Go home and get some rest." They had nothing, and Aster was becoming more and more lost to him. Linda was in the ambulance closest to him, wearing a sling and an oxygen mask. Zero was asleep at her feet. Payton sat across from her, rubbing her fingers through Zero's black fur.

When Linda saw him, she shifted closer to the door to speak with him. Zero lifted his head but didn't move, leaving Linda little space to get by him. "Where's Aster?" she asked.

"My snowmobile ran out of gas." It hadn't been his fault, but he felt foolish having to admit how he'd failed his daughter.

"The police have contacted all the neighboring towns. They've even enlisted the park service to cover the trails leading from here. I hope it's enough."

Vermont was a small state with a vast wilderness. Finding them would be difficult. He remembered Linda pointing the gun at Roman but hesitating. A heavy, anguished feeling threatened to drown him in fear. "You had a shot." He wished he could go back in time and holler at her to shoot. "You could have stopped him from taking her."

She leaned away from him. "That's not true. I didn't have a shot without risking Aster's life. And I would never put her in harm's way."

"Yet she's in the worst situation a person could be in. And Zero? Was he comfortable in the car while the world broke down into chaos? Why didn't you set him on Roman?" Why was Zero sitting in comfort while Aster was out there somewhere, cold, afraid and alone?

"Instead, you rushed off and decided to risk your life in a fire for a criminal?"

"Wait? You're blaming me for Aster being taken? I can't believe this." She shook her head, pulled off the oxygen mask and stood up, a bit off-balance but able to stand without assistance. She walked away from him, with Zero close behind on his leash.

Payton glared, her disappointment directed solely at him.

"I'm not blaming her," he said as he turned to chase down Linda. But he had. He'd fashioned a million reasons to blame her for Aster's abduction, when in reality, she'd been the one to delay his escape and had been the reason they had rescued her from the cabin. What an idiot. "Linda…" He came up next to her. "I'm sorry. It wasn't that. I'm terrified about Aster, and then I found out about you rushing into a burning building to save a murderer."

"I'm fine. And there's no proof Jeff killed anyone. He might be caught up in a lot of bad things, but that's not my judgment to make."

As she turned away from him, Officer Gates stepped between them and blocked access to her. It was no use trying to get by Maura. She was the toughest officer on the force.

Joe turned and walked back toward the ambulance, then circled around, following Linda.

When he got to her side, she continued walking away. "You need to get your ankle looked at."

"I'm fine. It's nothing that won't heal."

"It won't heal if you keep pushing it. Maybe you should take a few hours to put your feet up."

"I can't. I have to do something to find Aster, and my presence isn't wanted by the police."

"They're doing their best. I spoke to my dad. They have some leads on who Roman is and why he was in the area. The border guards, the state police and the police in the surrounding towns also are watching for him and Aster."

"It's not helping. There's got to be something more we could do." His words shot a barrage of demands that Linda didn't deserve. She was injured from helping him, yet he wanted more. "Are you okay?" he asked, not as an afterthought, but it was too late to sound as sincere as he meant.

"I've been worse," she said, staring off into the distance. Their connection, one that had seemed as tenuous as a thread when they'd driven up the mountain, seemed frayed apart. His behavior was to blame.

"That's not an answer," he responded. Seeing Linda lying on a stretcher all because she'd wanted to help him twisted his insides. He cared about her after all these years—so much so that he couldn't forgive himself for acting so ridiculous toward her when she only wanted to bring he and Aster closer. Perhaps she wasn't going to stick around, but their history connected them, and if he were half the man his mother had bragged about to everyone in earshot, he'd fight to keep some sort of relationship with her. The type of relationship at this point was unclear—maybe friendship, maybe something more—but he couldn't let her go again without telling her how much she meant to him. Time had changed them both, but time could also heal the wounds that had grown in their absence from one another.

As though she were reading his mind, she said, "There are so many bigger things going on. I want to figure out where Aster is. Until she's home safe, my own injuries seem insignificant."

"'Insignificant'?"

She nodded. "I'll manage my health just fine. I've done it before. I'm worried about Aster, too, but I know she's not out of reach. I can feel it."

After everything, she still maintained her faith that everything would work out. It made no sense. "I don't know how you keep seeing the best in every situation."

She managed a slight smile, but her lip quivered, as though caught in a deception. Had that been what kept her positive? Deceiving herself? "If you thought there was no hope to find Aster, what would you do?" she asked.

"If there was no hope? I don't know." But just imagining it nearly knocked him to the ground. There had to be a chance, even the smallest most improbable chance.

"I look at life as a series of problems," she explained. "Some small and insignificant, and some so large, they block out the sun. I can either allow the impossibility of any situation to bowl me over or I can roll up my sleeves and figure out a way to increase the odds in my favor. It doesn't always work. I've failed on too many occasions to remember. But one thing I'm sure of—I fail in everything where I believe there's no hope. When I have faith in God and myself, my odds increase. So why not believe? It's only upping our chances."

Her optimism trickled into his thoughts. This was yet another layer to a complicated woman. She was brave, caring, adventurous, funny, determined and smart. Although he was sure there were a lot of women like that—especially in the military—Linda, who had captivated him in high school, had again lodged herself into his heart.

He wanted to believe that she could fall back in love with him after so many years, despite his behavior when she'd left for the marines and just now after she'd rushed into a burning building to save a stranger. He shook his head. Winning her heart would be impossible. How could she like someone so critical of her? She also had bigger ambitions than him and Birch Glen. And he couldn't even love his own daughter properly. He had nothing to offer Linda.

Staring out toward the darkening forest, he wondered about Aster. Linda would tell him to have faith and trust that most things work out. Yet their adversary had been ruthless and smart and willing to do anything to escape.

"Where are you going?" he asked when she turned away from him.

"*We* are going to see Jeff," Linda said. "Apparently, he told Natie to have Payton pick her up. When she arrived with Aster, Natie had changed her mind, and Jeff wanted to speak to her. I find that strange and have many questions. First, how does Jeff know Payton? Second, why would they want to take Payton—and when she was freed, why take Aster? They want to use Aster and Payton as leverage because they could have escaped easily enough on the snowmobiles last night. It only brings more attention and intensity to the search. If we don't get good-enough answers out of him, we can go back to Payton and speak to her."

"He's unconscious."

"For now. They're waiting to medevac him, and until he's on the helicopter, he's ours."

Joe didn't say anything but took slow, tentative steps, minimizing his own injury as he passed an EMT. He didn't have the option of downtime to heal his ankle. They turned the corner and arrived at an ambulance with Jeff inside. Nick Sanders, the police department rookie, stood outside the door.

"Officer Sanders, any news on Aster?" Linda asked.

He shook his head. "We're working on it. Practically every unit in the state has someone on the case."

"That's good to know. Thanks," Joe said.

"I hope we get her back real soon."

Joe nodded. "I have faith we will." By saying the words, he felt movement forward toward finding his daughter. Perhaps faith worked that way—getting you to believe it would happen and setting out to help make it happen.

"I have a big favor to ask of you." Linda smiled at the officer, but her voice was all business.

Officer Sanders looked over them, then grimaced. "'A big favor'?"

"Five minutes with Jeff. You can even be in there with us. I promise I won't rough him up."

"Chief won't like it."

"If we get nothing, we say nothing. If we get information you can use, then you get the credit. Win-win."

He grimaced but stepped aside. "Five minutes, maximum. If any of those beepers go off, get out of there before anyone notices."

"Deal."

As Joe helped Linda inside the ambulance, her body shrank in the seat, her breathing became heavy and labored. If he hadn't seen her talking a mile a minute only moments before, he'd think she was at death's door. It was an act, but Joe didn't understand her endgame. Instead of questioning her, he trusted her tactics.

Jeff was on the stretcher, a bandage covering the gash on his head, black-and-blue marks on his face. He wore an oxygen mask. Not more than twenty-two or twenty-three years old, Jeff seemed too young to have done so much damage to one small village. Upon seeing Linda and Joe, he shifted uncomfortably. Officer Sanders's presence, however, kept him firmly in place.

Linda shifted toward him. "Hi, Jeff, I'm Linda and this is Joe, Aster's dad."

Jeff didn't say anything.

Linda coughed, nearly choking herself, something she hadn't done at all since taking off her own oxygen mask. "Do you recognize me?"

Jeff shrugged. He wouldn't exactly pipe up and say she was the person he fought at the isolated cabin.

"Do you remember anything from the fire?" Linda asked, talking without any expectation of an answer.

The room settled into an uncomfortable silence. Perhaps Jeff was debating talking, or perhaps he couldn't talk because of the smoke inhalation. Joe wanted to yell at him for taking his daughter, but he wasn't a fool. They needed Jeff to be on their side, and if he felt cornered, he'd remain silent.

Joe moved closer to Linda. "See that sling on her shoulder? She injured herself when she lifted you and helped you escape from the burning house. She risked her own life for yours."

Linda sat quietly on the bench inside the ambulance, appearing a bit more pained than she'd been in the other ambulance. The pitiful way she sat there must have tugged at Jeff's heart, because he nodded his head toward her and said, "Thanks."

She graced him with a hint of a smile. "I'm glad you're okay. Did you hurt anything on the fall?"

"No. Nothing sprained, nothing broken."

"Good. I was worried. I landed all wrong trying to escape after you. But my shoulder should be good as new after surgery."

He glanced at his hands, unable to meet her eyes. "Well, thanks again."

Joe couldn't leave it like that, and he was about to interrupt the rescue etiquette to demand where his daughter was being held.

Before he could say anything, Linda spoke again. "I understand you're going to be charged with kidnapping, arson and maybe murder. Did Officer Sanders read you your rights? Because you should know them," she said helpfully.

Jeff shrugged as though he didn't care what happened to him. The fight had either been knocked out of him in the fire or he'd been drugged for pain. Either way, he didn't seem like he'd be providing them with anything helpful.

"So far, you're an accessory to murder and kidnapping. I know the DA would see your case in a different light if you helped us find Roman and Aster. I can't imagine a prosecutor wanting to throw the book at you if you took a risk to help Aster the way I took a risk to help you. Your whole life is ahead of you. You deserve a second chance."

He turned to her, then looked up at Joe. There was a mountain of pain inside those eyes but many secrets as well. "I don't know where Roman is. He could be halfway back to Canada now."

"Toronto?" she asked.

"I think so."

Joe tried not to lose his focus to the panic of his daughter getting shipped over the border and lost to him forever. "Where are you from?" he asked Jeff.

"Attica."

"Where's that?"

"Outside of Buffalo."

So Roman had avoided this area and used flunkies to do his dirty work. Jeff had to be one of the smaller players in this mega-syndicate. Now that Joe had a better look at him, he recognized him from when Jeff had hung out mostly with high school–age kids over the past few months.

Linda slid closer to Jeff. He didn't seem to mind. Her approach was not threatening—more comforting, as though they shared a bond having fought through a fire together; although, from what Joe had heard, Linda had been the only one fighting. "If you don't mind, I just need to understand something. Why did you ask Natie to have Payton drive all the way up the mountain to take Natie home when there were several kids who were capable of driving her home already here?"

"Roman wanted to see her."

"Why? Do you know of a connection between them?" Joe asked.

Jeff turned his head away, his silence the loudest thing inside the ambulance.

Linda caught his attention again by rubbing her forehead as though she had a huge headache. "Did he say anything to her when she arrived?"

"I don't think he'd ever met her."

"That doesn't make sense. Why call her specifically?" Joe asked.

Jeff turned away. "I should call a lawyer."

At that, Officer Sanders stepped into the conversation. "You two need to leave."

Joe helped her out of the ambulance, and Officer Sanders shut the door and stood back in front of it.

"Thanks for the five minutes," Linda said.

"I don't know what you're talking about." He gave her a brief wave. "Take care of yourself, Linda."

"I will. Maybe you should have the Dixon family moved to the police station for a few hours while you sort things through. Get the family under protective custody."

"I'll call the chief and suggest it. See you later." Officer Sanders went on his radio and called in the information he'd heard.

They walked away in silence as the flood of new details rushed through Joe's mind. Roman had wanted Payton? Aster had been caught in the cross fire.

"I should head to the Dixon house." Joe needed a new focus.

The injured and distressed Linda who had spoken to Jeff disappeared as quickly as she'd arrived. "We should speak to Payton first. Get her to answer why Roman wanted her to drive to the Primley house."

Chapter Eighteen

The distant hum of helicopter blades made everyone at the fire take notice. The noise grew until a medevac helicopter came into view. The police waved them over to a field at the side of the house.

The helicopter came closer, hovering above them. Linda felt the need to guide them in, as she would have in a military operation, but her lungs weren't filling with air as normal, and she was dizzy. Although she'd faked her ailments when visiting Jeff, the smoke had taken a toll on her, and she could barely catch her breath with so much activity. Zero barked and pulled on the leash as the sound of the helicopter overwhelmed the area. Her arm hurt too much to reach out to him, and she fell to her knees.

A team in green jumpsuits hopped out of the side door of the helicopter. One of the team members strode over to Officer Gates as the others rushed toward Jeff. One medic approached Linda.

"Hi, I'm Dr. Johnson. Can I speak with you?" the older woman asked.

Linda nodded, but when she tried to speak, she coughed instead. Dr. Johnson and a man in a similar flight suit tried to position her onto a stretcher, but she fought them off.

"It's not me you're here for. It's Jeff." She pointed to the ambulance guarded by the police. She couldn't go to the hospital; there was too much to do. Aster wasn't home yet. And Joe was trying to restrain a panicked Zero.

Linda needed to get to him. Zero hated helicopters, and the stress might cause him to bolt. He pulled to get to her side, barking, all agitated. She wanted to reach out to him, to assure him that everything would be all right, that they'd be together soon, but the noise of the helicopter blades drowned out any ability to calm him.

Jeff was on a stretcher being pushed into the helicopter. He was unconscious again, or maybe they'd given him something to make the trip easier. A few officers moved Linda and several firefighters back to allow for more clearance around the helicopter. They pushed her farther away from Zero, who was fighting as hard as he could to get free.

Joe could barely restrain Zero. Linda had mentioned her dog's fear of helicopters, and here he was, panicked at Joe's side, with Linda on the other side, out of their line of sight. The dog pulled back on the lead, shaking his head to get free. Joe squatted down, trying to calm him, but he continued shaking and barking. As the helicopter took off, Zero fought him some more.

Officer Gates came over and told him he was wanted at the police station. She offered to take Zero back to Linda, but as she reached out for the leash, Zero pulled free, running as fast as he could straight into the forest, following the flight of the helicopter. Joe couldn't deal with any more trauma. He couldn't deal with anything. The only thing he could think of doing was run after Zero, screaming his name.

Linda caught up to him and held his arm. "Stop. You'll only scare him. Follow Officer Faruk back to town. I'll wait here with the firefighters to see if he comes back."

The sun wouldn't remain up for too much longer. Then cold and darkness would swoop in and put Zero further at risk. Aster was at risk too. He had to go. Maybe the police had news about her location. "Okay. Call me if you find him."

"No problem." She waved and stepped farther into the woods, following the dog's footsteps as Joe returned to the parking area and got into his Jeep.

He waved to Ryan in the vehicle ahead of him, and they both began the journey back to town. The house was burning, his daughter was gone, Linda and Zero were going back into the forest. The losses overwhelmed him. He had to do something—but first, he'd head to the police station.

He followed Ryan's cruiser down the driveway in his Jeep. Driving alone allowed him to think about everything that had happened. He'd been harsh with Linda and couldn't begin to forgive himself.

When he'd arrived at the police station, Vince greeted him. "How's Linda?" he asked.

"Okay, I guess." His thoughts in a haze, he only had so much optimism, and at this point, he had no faith in anything or anyone. "She's up at the Primley place." He didn't want to mention Zero gone missing. "She took in a lot of smoke in the fire but is otherwise fine." She had to be fine.

Vince nodded. "Good. The chief is worried about her."

"Any word on Aster?" Joe asked.

Vince shook his head. Although his official title was receptionist, he was a former officer injured while pulling over a drunk driver. He had more knowledge and understanding of the backgrounds on cases than all the rookies combined. "No location. But the chief tracked down information on Roman. His full name is Roman Laskin. He has an operation out of Toronto and is wanted at the border but keeps sliding through, delivering lethal drugs to small communities across Vermont, Upstate New York and New Hampshire. A multimillion-dollar operation. He won't be able to get through any regular border crossing tonight, especially with Aster. How are you doing?"

"I'm not," Joe admitted, his bravado gone, his thoughts a whirlwind of doubt.

"Understandable. Why don't you go back to the inn, and we'll inform you when we get any new information."

"You want me to sit tight and wait?" He couldn't just stare at a wall when his daughter was missing. He'd wasted enough time being unable to look for her.

"Until we have new information, there's no other choice. We don't know whether Roman is headed to the border or will stay on the run. Chief asked two rangers to remain staked out at the cabin Linda told us about, but it's a big wilderness. We can't cover the entire national park, never mind all the adjoining areas. You'll need rest if you want to help Aster. Being overtired and overwhelmed is a useless combination. Go home."

Joe merely nodded. When he returned to the inn, he nodded off for a few moments and woke with a different perspective now that his brain fog had burned off. He called the police for an update, but they had nothing new to offer him. He stared at the entrance, with its large wooden door. Guests filled up the place, and he couldn't care. All he wanted was his daughter back. He had to do something. There was one person in town he trusted to have his and Aster's best interests at heart: Linda. He knew it down to the soles of feet and in the deepest chasms of his heart.

Chapter Nineteen

Linda's heart hurt even more than her body. Zero ran away when the helicopter took off. He was not a wilderness dog; he was a working dog with a fairly cushy lifestyle. Surviving in the mountains in the dead of winter would be challenging for any animal who called the Green Mountains home. For Zero, who'd grown up and trained in Southern California, the terrain was a new experience. Linda had no idea how Zero would adapt. He'd been by her side for so much of the past four years. A tear fell.

Her father arrived on the scene, dressed in his uniform with a heavy black wool coat that fell just below his knees. "How are you feeling?"

With his graying hair and the slightly rounded stomach that had appeared soon after he accepted the administrative position as chief of police, he seemed older. He'd mentioned to her that he was hoping to retire in the next two years, but she couldn't envision him without that dark blue uniform he'd worn since she was in diapers, and she couldn't imagine the town without him.

"Why are you up here?" she asked.

"I wanted to interview Jeff, see if he has any information that can help us."

"You're too late. He's probably already in a cozy bed at the hospital."

"I wanted to check on you too."

"I'm fine." She preferred that her father focus on Aster's whereabouts. "Any news about Aster?"

"None yet, but I promise I'll keep you in the loop."

"Thanks."

"You don't look fine." He sounded worried.

"I'm back to square one. My shoulder is all messed up again." Her throat hurt as she spoke, but that was nothing compared to the pain of watching one's child being taken by a thug. "I'm glad Payton's okay, but I can't help but torture myself for allowing Roman to escape with Aster."

He leaned against his car. His expression carried more rain than sunshine. "You're never satisfied with anything less than perfection. Stop being hard on yourself. You're a hero. You helped rescue Aster and Payton at the cabin. You stopped Jeff, a drug dealer, from poisoning the town. And you gave enough of a description of Roman that the state police have photos of him circulating all over social media."

She sighed. It meant something for her father finally to acknowledge her efforts, but this wasn't the time to soak up parental encouragement.

"What do you know about Roman?" she asked him.

He rubbed a hand over his temple. "He's a known distributor. To my knowledge, he'd only travel to meet with small-town dealers if they're insubordinate or stealing from him. The fact that this situation has grown so out of control makes me second-guess my efforts at stopping dealers in the area."

"Jeff blended into the town, becoming friendly with the most popular kids and the richest part-timers. You would never have found out unless one of the kids snitched on him. You have him in custody—that's a start. My question is whether Roman has any reason besides Jeff to return to Birch Glen." She wanted Roman stopped, but her biggest concern was him fleeing over the border with Aster.

"There is one thing we aren't sure about," her father said. "Why were they so fixated on Payton and Aster?"

"Payton and Aster might have heard the gunshot, and they saw Noah fall to the ground. Roman was holding the gun. They're witnesses to a murder."

"Wrong place at the wrong time. Too bad these kids couldn't have stayed in town."

Linda shook her head at her father's assumption. "Payton and Aster didn't come up here because of the party. Natie called Payton to pick her up, but it wasn't Natie's idea to call Payton. It was Jeff's or maybe Roman's idea."

Her father shrugged. "We've been unable to interview Jeff. He became unconscious again on the flight and hasn't woken up yet."

Linda was hesitant to tell him she'd already spoken to him. One word from him, and she'd be shut out of the investigation. "If you draw a line between Jeff, Roman, Payton and Natie, you might have enough information to track him down."

He nodded. "I'll have someone question Natie again and sit down with Payton to gain a bigger picture of how she ended up there with Aster." He reached out and squeezed her hand. "Have you located Zero?"

"Not yet." Just thinking about her dog caused the knot in her gut to tighten so much, she could barely stand.

"I'll have the team watch for him as they work. And, honey, go easy on Joe. He's carrying a lot of guilt over his wife's death. He must feel terrible the way this rescue attempt is going."

"What do you mean? I thought it was a car accident."

"She drove out in a storm to make Joe's favorite dinner. She never made it home." Her father waved at Linda, indicating he needed to take a request on his radio, then walked away.

Linda remained frozen, contemplating the mountain of guilt Joe carried with him. No wonder he was over-protective of Aster.

Chapter Twenty

Knowing her father and the police were fully focused on getting Aster back, Linda returned to searching for Zero for another two hours, tracking his paw prints until they disappeared under the swirl of fallen snow off the surrounding trees. Fatigue made every decision agonizing. She wanted to continue looking, but the cold cut into her lungs and she no longer could feel her toes. She returned to what was left of the chalet. The firefighters had stopped the fire from overwhelming the whole house. The half of the house where the kitchen had been was destroyed, but the other half where she'd found Jeff appeared intact.

A familiar Jeep sat by a police cruiser, with Joe in the driver's seat. He was dressed the same as the last time she'd seen him, with what seemed like fifty extra pounds of stress on his back.

"It always makes me sad to see something that had been so beautiful destroyed," she said to him as he exited the vehicle.

Joe shook his head. "That fire nearly took you with it. I'm just grateful you're okay." He squeezed her hand, making her heart beat a bit faster. "I know this seems like it's coming out of left field after all the time we've been apart, but you mean something to me. Not just because of our past." He cleared his throat. "I care about you."

She let out a sigh and smiled. "Thanks." She'd never been one to receive compliments well, but this one sat deep inside her and filled her up. It had been a long time since someone besides her parents had truly valued her, and sometimes she believed they were merely doing their parental duty.

"I've hit a dead end on finding Aster. So now what?" he asked.

"First, believe in us finding Aster so much that she almost appears right before your eyes."

That wasn't the answer he wanted. "You're confident about using this technique for Zero too?" he replied, then added, "I'm sorry. That was uncalled for. It's as though my fear has overridden my empathy."

Linda nodded. She'd seen many people swamped with concern for a family member when she'd been with the military police. "Zero is smart and brave and prefers curling up in blankets on my couch to sleeping in the cold, so I'm sure he'll find his way back. Let's focus on Aster for a bit." She sighed and turned around, pushing her darkest thoughts away.

The police chief's car was parked near three fire engines, two from Birch Glen and one from a neighboring town. The water tank inside one of the engines contained hundreds of gallons of water, a necessity for off-the-grid houses, where any pond or outdoor water source would be frozen over with a thick layer of ice. An ambulance lingered for any emergencies during the fire fighting. On the far end of the parking lot, two more police cars and…her mother's car?

Linda shook her head in disbelief. Her mother, a woman who wore heels each day and preferred a pool to a pond, stood with two firefighters. She had probably taught them in school.

"Mom? What are you doing here?" Linda walked over to her and hugged her tight.

"Your father told me about Zero, and I knew you wouldn't be able to concentrate until he came back to you. The fire and police departments have their hands full with everything else going on, so I drove up to see if I could help find him."

"Thank you so much, but you didn't have to do that." She smiled to herself. Her mother was a tiger mom toward her and apparently toward Zero too.

"Has someone put out any food for him?" Linda asked.

"No need."

"What do you mean?"

Her mother pointed toward a fire engine. Zero, wrapped in a blanket, was in the driver's seat, eating something from the firefighter sitting next to him.

"Zero!" Linda called out.

He turned and began to shake the whole truck, trying to get out. The firefighter opened the door, and Zero jumped down and ran over to her, wiggling side to side and nearly knocking her off her feet.

"Oh, sweetheart," Linda said, wiping tears from her face. "I am so sorry the helicopter scared you. I was so worried about you."

Zero didn't seem to be holding a grudge. His tail motored back and forth like a propeller, and he pressed tight into her as though sticking to her would keep her at his side. She knelt and rubbed his fur. He was cold but healthy. She kissed the top of his head and burst into fresh tears, the relief flooding through her.

"How did you find him?" she asked her mother.

"Zero scampered into the yard about ten minutes ago. He returned to the last place he saw you. I tried to call you but couldn't get a signal."

"I've been out looking for him." She remained squatted, hugging him. "Are you hungry, Zero?"

"Probably not. They did a food run, and he somehow ended up with two hamburgers and a small order of french fries."

Normally, Linda would have been horrified by him eating junk food, but he appeared healthy and happy, and she couldn't fault anyone for caring for him in the best way they thought at the time.

"Have you heard anything about Aster?" her mother asked, looking up at Joe.

"Nothing." He turned around as her father approached them.

"Any news on Roman since last we spoke?" she asked her father.

He shook his head. "It's like he disappeared into thin air. We've placed checkpoints up and down the roads.

He might be bunkering down for a while until everything blows over."

For some reason, his theory didn't sit right with her. Roman had been desperate to find whatever was in the house—this house and maybe the cabin where they'd rescued Aster and Payton. She looked over at what was left of it. Roman was a drug dealer, and she just so happened to have a drug-sniffing dog at her side. It might be a lot to push him after such a strenuous twenty-four hours, but Aster's life was on the line.

While her father and mother consoled Joe, she went to the fire truck where Zero had been sitting. Someone had taken his harness off, and she found it on the floor of the passenger seat—a wet mess but the best indicator to him that it was time to work. "Sorry, buddy, but we have one extra task to do here before we leave."

He licked her face as she bent over to tighten the straps. Labradors were bred to hunt, and they seemed happiest working. Same with her.

Joe walked up beside her. "Ready to go?"

As long as Aster was missing, he'd be pushing to keep moving, even if he didn't know where it was he was going. She understood the feeling, but they had run out of ideas where to search, and right now, she had a chance to maybe add something to the investigation.

"Jeff had been staying here, and their presence at the party had annoyed Noah. Roman wouldn't have made an appearance in front of so many people if he hadn't wanted something inside this house. That's why they returned. Something he didn't want anyone else discovering. He was willing to burn the house down in order to hide it. If I'm right, we might have a better understanding of what his next move will be."

"You want to search a burning house?"

"The fire's out mostly, and I'd only search areas deemed somewhat safe." If Zero located something useful, law enforcement could anticipate Roman's next move. "We need more information to track down Roman, and I have a gut feeling it's in there." She pointed to the house.

From the look on Joe's face, he wasn't in agreement with her, but she had to trust her intuition, her training and her experience, unless of course the police chief blocked her.

Chapter Twenty-One

$\sim$

Linda made her way to the far side of the house with Zero trekking next to her. Joe was in charge of keeping her father away from her. Once he figured out what she was going to do, he wouldn't be too happy about it. He'd always been protective of her, but seeing her enter a smoldering building might be too much. A few firefighters were pulling burnt wood off the siding that could reignite. A ladder leaned against the house—a ladder that would have been helpful when she'd been trying to escape the blaze. As fate would have it, Tom was still there. He appeared far more disheveled, exhaustion steaming from every visible part of him.

"Tom, you're just the person I wanted to see." Linda went over to him. Zero trotted at her side.

"Your father has been swarming all over this scene. He wasn't impressed with you rescuing Jeff. He wanted his daughter safe and on the ground. I tried to explain to him that you were already up there and leaving Jeff behind would have been cold-blooded, but he's your dad, so who am I to challenge him?" he said. "Anyway, I was impressed. How are you doing?"

"Better than before. Sore shoulder but nothing too bad." She was under-exaggerating her injuries because to pull off what she was about to ask him, he'd have to believe she was in far better condition than she was.

"Tom." Joe came up next to them—no father in sight, but that didn't mean he wouldn't show up.

"Joe. Sorry about Aster. I'm praying for her."

Joe shut down. The reminder of Aster's situation must have been a sucker punch. It was a helpless situation to be in, but if Tom helped her out, maybe they wouldn't be so in the dark about her location.

Linda interrupted them. Standing in knee-deep grief would help no one. "I was hoping you could help us. It's about finding Aster."

Tom looked over at Joe, who was still lost in his thoughts. He'd always been close with him and probably watched Aster grow up without her mother, as the whole town had. It was enough to make anyone extra protective of her. "What do you need?"

"Roman was looking for something, tearing that bedroom apart." She pointed to the window she'd jumped from. "Maybe Noah had more involvement in Roman's operation than just offering up a house. He'd lived here with Jeff for several months. Maybe there's a computer with files or Noah's cell phone up there. Something that could help us find Aster."

He shrugged. "What can I do?"

"Can you help me scan the room for any evidence left

behind and let Zero search for traces of a narcotic? Jeff had been running the operation out of here for months."

"Your father would never approve of that."

"I didn't realize the fire department had to follow all the directives of the police. Isn't this your jurisdiction?" The police–fire rivalry had been going on for years between her father and Fire Chief Greg Getty. Getty hated when Linda's father stepped over the line in responding to a fire, trying to run the response. Linda understood all about power struggles and intended to use every bit of ammunition she could to get what she wanted. She had one focus, and that was Aster. She'd manipulate everything in her power to find her.

It seemed to work. Tom glanced up at the burnt structure, smoke still streaming from some of the walls; the entire roof over the kitchen had collapsed. He looked at the window she'd jumped from. "There aren't too many stable areas left inside. Maybe that room and the next one down the hall."

There was a chance they'd find nothing, but she had to try. The risk was more than worth it. "Let's do it. For Aster."

Joe's eyed widened with realization. "Wait. That's too dangerous."

"We might find something with Zero's help." She spoke with certainty even though doubts poked at her. They had no other options. "If Noah or Jeff hid all the drug-related materials together, which dealers tend to do, then it would be inside and most likely in Noah's bedroom. It had been trashed during the party and Roman and Jeff returned to it the next day."

Joe shook her head. "You're injured."

"So what? I can do the job and maybe help your daughter." She turned to Tom. "Please, let me do what I was trained to do."

He looked around, then told her to meet him in the front of the house at the command post they'd set up earlier. The fire chief was in his car, looking over notes. Tom spoke to him, pointing and gesticulating. She didn't interrupt, understanding the power dynamics in this situation. It would be best if Tom fought this battle for her. Her father was standing with a large radio, screaming commands into it. Linda remained hidden from her father's view.

Tom waved her back behind the house where her father couldn't see them. Tom then called another firefighter over. Linda had seen her at the coffee shop on many occasions, drinking hot chocolate and avoiding coffee. Amy, the youngest firefighter in town, had just graduated the fire academy. Tom sized her up and then looked at Linda. "Okay, Amy, I need you to take photos of the initial blaze site. I wouldn't usually ask you this, but I also need your helmet and your jacket…and gloves and boots." He paused and faced Linda. "No. This isn't going to work. You have no training in this equipment."

"I have some training." Not specifically in firefighting, but Linda had to appear competent to pull this off.

At first, Amy appeared annoyed to be called back from what she'd been doing. The youngest firefighter always got sent off for crowd control, picture-taking or some other less risky assignment.

Tom didn't seem to care about her feelings. "Amy,

Linda isn't going in to fight the fire. She needs to locate something—anything—that will help locate Aster. It's now or never."

"I wouldn't ask if I didn't think I could help Aster," Linda said to her. "If either of you get in trouble, I'll take the blame. All of it."

Amy pulled off one of her gloves and handed it to Linda. "Aster is two years behind me in high school. Super quiet but a good kid. Sure, I'll help."

Linda thanked her. She struggled into the pants, which were a tad tight for her, as were the bunker boots, but the gear was necessary to complete the task safely—as long as she ignored the pain caused by the extra weight on her shoulder from the heavy jacket.

Chief Getty walked over to her and handed her a new self-contained breathing apparatus. She'd trained on these in the military. "These we never share. Good luck."

"Thanks."

Tom climbed up first to determine if it even was safe for them go up there. Linda never would have asked him to risk his own safety if Aster's life wasn't on the line. He felt the floor to ensure Zero could stand on it without dog boots to protect his feet since she didn't have any with her. She hated putting him at risk too. He'd been through so much. As she climbed up, she promised herself that she'd abort the task if it was too much for him.

Once Tom gave the all clear, Linda indicated for Zero to climb the ladder. One firefighter on each side held the ladder steady. Too bad they couldn't get a truck with a bucket into the back. She eased him up one rung at a time. He hesitated, but she coaxed him, and soon they were both standing inside Noah's room.

"Stay away from this area," Tom said, indicating toward the wall where the door had been on fire. "Fire still could be smoldering inside the walls."

Linda looked at the fire damage and the rush of water that had blasted through to control the blaze. The whole house was beyond salvage; it was a disaster area. This task would have to be handled quickly to protect Zero.

Her dog sniffed the ground, probably getting his bearings in the room. Linda made a circle to indicate the room and said "Where's Mickey?" Her voice sounded muffled from inside the helmet, but Zero reacted to the command.

He immediately began sniffing. He lifted his head and checked the drawers and around the bed, into the hamper... He showed no interest in any of those areas. When the dog got to the closet, he pawed at the door. Tom went over and opened the door for them. Zero's posture changed, and he froze in place for a moment, his focus on the closet. He went inside, sat and looked at Linda. His alert.

She knelt and shifted away dirty clothes and random sneakers and boots on the closet floor but couldn't see what he was indicating toward. "Where is it?"

He refocused. His nose found something behind the door. He sat again. Linda went inside the closet and pushed on the wall. Sure enough, a portion of the wall not visible from the room slid open and exposed an opening. Something was in there.

"Can I reach inside?" she asked Tom.

"If you step back, I'll reach inside."

Linda backed herself and Zero into the room and allowed Tom into the closet.

He checked for hot spots, then reached inside and pulled out a shoebox. "Bingo." He opened it, and sure enough, three small packets of blue capsules, a wad of money secured with an elastic band and various scraps of paper were inside.

She praised Zero and gave him lots of hugs. He needed to receive a reward for his efforts to know he'd found what she'd asked him, but his normal reward—a squeaky armadillo tug toy—was back at her house.

"Is anything else in there?" Linda asked, as this was her only chance to get every possible bit of evidence.

He reached inside again, then shook his head. "We should go."

She nodded.

They went to the window, attached the leash to the front and back of the dog's harness, and lowered him from the second floor to a group of firefighters waiting for them. Then she climbed out to the ladder. Partway down, Tom handed her the shoebox and climbed down after her.

Her feet secure on the ground, she hugged Zero again, the adrenaline of working an investigation and handling her dog tempered the pain in her shoulder and the ache in her heart over Aster's disappearance. She removed the helmet and took a breath of the crisp winter air.

She carried the box away from the crowd of firefighters and found some water she could give to Zero and drink for herself. She hid by one of the engines to strip off the jacket and gloves, then handed the helmet to Amy. Amy swapped back Roman's coat. Linda took that opportunity to shuffle through the contents of the box, ignoring the money and the packets of pills.

The scraps of paper had her interest. One included a list of names with possible debts owed; another had a hand-drawn map of Vermont, with eight areas delineated in a rainbow of colors. This area had been outlined and colored in with green—not a solid forest green but a fluorescent green, as though the maker of the chart had seven colored crayons and one fluorescent pen. Birch Glen and the surrounding area glowed.

The list proved far more useful. Seven people were listed under Rutland, a far-bigger town with a far-bigger police force. For Birch Glen and the surrounding areas, there were four names: Johnson (Glennondale), Frasier (Braxfield), (Primley), and Dixon (Shiver). Primley probably stood for Jeff or Noah or both, so Linda focused on Dixon. Perhaps that was why Jeff had told Natie to call Payton and have her drive up there: she was involved with Roman and Jeff in the local drug trade. But that made no sense after speaking to Payton. She didn't have a clue who Jeff or Roman were.

Linda's father approached, his frown painting the situation with his judgement. "I don't think I've ever been so disappointed in you."

His statement felt like a slap in the face. "I'm sure I've let you down multiple times over the years." This wasn't the place to confront his inability to see her as a capable adult. Instead, she showed the list to her father.

"You can yell me at me later for going back inside, but I think this is the best chance to find Aster."

"This list? You risked your life for this?" He didn't even look at it. "I understand you want to help Joe, but you not only put yourself at risk, but you also placed Tom in harm's way with your escapades. You're not trained for any of this."

"Not trained? What do you think I was doing these past years?"

"Not rushing into burning buildings."

"The building wasn't burning." Not really. The majority of the flames were out—and besides, she'd taken a calculated risk for the benefit of someone else. "This list could lead us to Aster."

"There is no 'us' in this. You're unemployed, and I have a whole town to care for."

"Fine. You should send an officer to the Dixon house."

"I don't have the staff to check on every one of your theories." His insult burned. He shifted his attention to one of his detectives, who had found a weapon in one of the burned-out rooms: a twelve-gauge hunting shotgun, one that was common in this area. "See if the lab can locate a serial number. We might get a lead."

The detective nodded and walked away.

Linda shook her head. He was jumping at all the wrong evidence. If he wasn't so focused on proving her incompetent, he'd realize it. The shotgun was probably registered to the owner of the house. People hunted here, and shotguns were far more effective in hunting than for personal defense. A drug dealer would carry something portable, not something with a two-foot barrel. She had gone against drug dealers smart enough to transport drugs into a heavily guarded military installation. This was her expertise, despite what her father said.

"I would appreciate it if you didn't appear so outwardly dismissive of my orders." He glanced around, more aware of the other officers near him than of Linda.

"If you just listen to me…"

He waved her to stop. "I'm done with you right now. I have work to do, and you should be resting. Go home."

Linda relied a lot on her intuition backed with a large dose of common sense. And her intuition demanded she head back to the Dixon house. Her father wouldn't approve of her continued investigation, so she didn't tell him.

"Fine. Joe and I are driving down to the village. Can you call us if you hear anything?" As she spoke, her mother arrived.

"Liz, please get Linda to rest." Her father was interrupted by another officer and walked away.

"I have a turkey stew in the Crock-Pot," her mother said to her and Joe. "Get some nourishment. The best thing for the both of you is to rest. You look as though you've come through a war zone."

Linda shook her head. "Not yet. Not until Aster is as safe as Zero."

Her mother hugged her again, avoiding Linda's hurt shoulder. "I'm so proud of what you've done. I can't even imagine all the heroic things you've accomplished over the years that I don't know about. Take care of yourself." She kissed her cheek and released her, then she turned to Joe. "And you take care of my baby. Len will find your daughter. I'm sure of it."

"Seriously, Mom?" It was so like her mother to compliment her, then insult her in the next breath.

"Linda is far more capable in these situations than I am." Joe gave a half smile, one that would appease a woman who had spoken from the heart but missed the depth of pain he was under.

Joe leaned against a fire engine, breathing in the cold air and trying to clear the shadows from his thoughts. Watching Linda with her mother and her dog, he remembered all those days he'd lingered in their kitchen, enjoying a family that seemed more conventional than his. His included only him and his mother. His father had taken off when he'd entered high school. Not that she'd done a bad job, but it was an effort. She had no help and rarely rested. Perhaps that was where he'd picked up his work habits, always another thing to accomplish before he could spend time with Aster. He hoped it wasn't too late to change that. There were so many things he wanted to change. First, he had to find her.

Linda waved goodbye to her mother, then signaled to Joe with a twitch of her head toward the Jeep that she wanted to leave. The movement was subtle but assured. She had a plan, and Joe had no reason to go against it. As a teenager, Linda had filled his life with love and belonging, but she'd returned different. She had a maturity in her worldview, a confidence, an inner strength. He wanted this version of Linda in his life. In fact, he couldn't imagine life with anyone else. But this was not the time to think about their future—not until Aster's future was secure.

He watched her as she opened the door to let Zero inside. Her demeanor had changed when she saw her dog. It was as though someone had lifted a thousand-pound weight off her shoulders. Or added eighty pounds of adoring animal into her heart. Dogs were family. Joe had owned a dog growing up, a Havanese his mother had named Sadie. Sadie hadn't been trained to do anything more than hike with a boy in the woods and eat the food that fell from the counter. She held all Joe's secrets, comforted him with a lick on the face, acted as his constant companion no matter what. She'd been like a guardian angel to him, like Zero seemed to Linda.

Zero stared out the window from the back seat, his tail wagging in an almost-circular motion. He then settled into a tight ball and sighed.

"It looks like he's forgiven me for bringing him to a place where helicopters land." She reached back and rubbed his head. The tough-as-steel marine had tears in her eyes.

"How could he be angry with you? You had no choice. You couldn't refuse to let it land. I'm sure he sensed that."

The dog pressed his head into her hand and closed his eyes, the trauma of the day seeming easier to handle with Linda back by his side. Joe felt the same way.

Chapter Twenty-Two

With Linda safe at his side, Joe's confidence grew as he drove down the mountain. They could find Aster. They'd done so before without the use of a car or an entire police force. Just the act of driving eased his mind, even if it turned out to be a dead end. He couldn't just sit around waiting for the police to rescue her. The thought of all the things that she could be going through enraged him. If it weren't for Linda, he would have broken down hours ago. He wasn't sure what Linda's game plan was, but he knew she had Aster's well-being prioritized above all else.

"We're not going to your house, are we?" he asked Linda.

"I'm not hungry, but we can stop there if you need food."

He shook his head. "I don't think I'll be able to eat again until Aster is found." His stomach was so full of knots, he could barely breathe properly. "Should I head to the Dixons?"

"Yes, but drive to Shiver Cabin first."

"I was there earlier. It was vacant."

Linda shrugged. "If Roman wanted something in the Primley place and couldn't find it, perhaps he'll look for it at Shiver Cabin. The cabin was listed right after Dixon on the list. My father couldn't mind me checking on an abandoned cabin he claims he has no interest in."

Interfering in a police investigation could land a person in jail, but checking a few leads without getting in the way of a police investigation? That seemed perfectly legal. And Linda would know if they were stepping over the line.

"Officer Gates said the Dixons are still at the police station," she added. "We can check the cabin and then head to their house afterward. Something tells me that the party was moved because of George."

"George Dixon?" he asked.

"Roman had no idea who Payton was, so she wasn't connected to him. Her brother, on the other hand, had his tires slashed and didn't want to leave the safety of his house. Too coincidental to be a coincidence. We can check in at the Red Pepper Inn first if you need a break."

"If I even have an inn to go back to. The reviewer from *Yankee* magazine needs to give us an amazing review for us to survive this next season, but I can't care about any of that until Aster's back. So, Shiver Cabin it is."

She placed a hand over Joe's. The warmth of her fingers eased some of his strain. "One step at a time."

They parked a hundred meters from the cabin, behind a curve in the road, so the Jeep wouldn't be visible from the cabin. No lights inside were on.

"Should we circle it once?" he asked.

She nodded and led Zero a few steps in front of her. The Dixons' RAV4 was parked in back.

Linda looked inside the windows of the car. "Bingo. This is all making sense. It wasn't Jeff who was keeping something from Roman—it was George, but George refused to meet him. That's why he wouldn't go to the party. Roman slashed his tires in warning. Roman would never let anyone get away with stealing from him. George either had to come up with the drugs or the cash. Maybe someone stole it from him. In order to get George's attention, Roman took Payton as collateral."

"George didn't seem all that concerned about her when we were at their house earlier." Joe's respect for him fell to nothing. Anyone who could so easily hand over a family member—or anyone, for that matter—was not a person Joe wanted living in Birch Glen.

The distant crunch of snow caught his attention. Zero turned toward the woods behind the house.

"Over here." Joe led Linda behind the car.

Linda pulled out the gun she'd had at the Primley place. "Do you know how to use this?"

"You know I do. I've been going to the range since I was in high school." He was better with hunting rifles and shotguns, but he could handle the gun. He took it and did a quick safety check, keeping it in his hand, ready for anything. "Do you have a weapon?"

She nodded and glanced down at Zero.

The footsteps came closer. They were coming from the forest on the far side of the cabin.

"It's them," Joe said, shifting forward.

"Wait. I only see one person. Roman."

He came into full view, wearing Linda's jacket, which was far too small for him. He must have taken it off Aster. That would mean Aster was freezing cold somewhere, or worse. The thought froze the blood in Joe's veins. As Roman entered the yard, he ducked behind a tree. Before Linda and Joe could stop him, Roman lifted his gun and shot through a cabin window. Glass shattered and someone screamed.

Joe stepped forward and pointed the gun at Roman. Roman, still protected by the tree, turned toward him, and Joe hesitated. Linda stood behind him, holding Zero, his low growl in the background.

"Come out," he called out to Roman.

"You'll have to kill me." He pointed the muzzle toward Linda. "You seem to have trouble keeping the women in your life safe."

"Where's Aster?"

"I guess you'll never know if you kill me."

So much could go wrong. Joe froze, waiting for something—a sign, a shout, a shot. The shot Linda never took to save Aster up at the Primley place flashed through his mind. She'd been in this situation; she could have taken a shot, but what if she'd missed and hit Aster? It wouldn't have been worth it.

Roman gestured to Zero. "That mutt needs to die." He shot at Zero, missing, and caused the dog to pull Linda almost off her feet.

Joe shot at him to protect the others, but purposely missed by inches. Bark splintered off the tree. He ducked back down and watched as Linda charged out from behind him toward the tree, sending Zero off leash toward the tree in the opposite direction. The multiple angles from which they attacked Roman caused him to lose focus and step around the tree. When he lifted his gun again, it was aimed directly at Linda.

Joe took the shot, striking Roman in the chest. His body pitched into the bush behind him; the gun in his hand slipped into the snow. Joe rushed forward.

Linda crouched beside Roman, taking the gun away from him.

"Check in the cabin for Aster," she said. Her focus remained on keeping Roman down.

Joe rushed around to the front of the cabin and pushed on the door. It opened without effort. "Aster?" he called out.

No answer.

He ran from the main room, a dusty graveyard of wooden furniture and beer bottles, to the back of the cabin, where there was a kitchen. The window had been shattered by Roman's first shot. On the floor, George lay in a pool of blood. He appeared conscious, the blood coming from his upper arm.

"Where's Aster?" Joe asked him.

"I don't know." He shook his head with effort and shut his eyes.

The distant scream of sirens gave Joe the confidence to leave George on the ground while he looked for his only child. He opened every cabinet door, the closet door and a wooden trunk. There weren't many places for her to hide. The police rushed through the door, and an ambulance team followed.

George tried to get up but fell back with a howl of agony. Joe wanted to care but couldn't until Aster was safe.

Chapter Twenty-Three

Between Linda, Zero and a serious gunshot wound to the chest, Roman wasn't going anywhere. She knelt beside him, over a foot farther than his arm span, with the gun pointed toward his chest. Just in case. "Where's Aster?"

"Dead or soon dead." He coughed up blood, but his eyes stayed on Linda's face.

If Joe had found her in the cabin, the news would have traveled outside. She was tempted to strangle Roman until he told her Aster's location, but there was too much risk involved. Besides, that wasn't how she operated.

The police arrived, but she remained with them at his side, hopeful he might give away even a hint about Aster's location. The medics rushed forward. In a moment, she'd be barred from the area and from Roman. She had one more chance to get anything from him.

"There she is. Thank God." She looked back into the forest where he'd come from, pretending to see Aster emerge. Linda prayed for even the slightest movement from him that would give away her location.

Roman arched his neck but was unable to lift his head more than an inch from the ground. He didn't reply.

The swarm of professionals pushed her from his side. She stepped back with Zero. Joe rushed toward her. His expression showed not one bit of hope, but she had more than enough to spare.

Officer Faruk came up to them. "What happened?"

"The idiot who took my daughter shot into the cabin and then at Linda. I defended her and later found George wounded by a gunshot inside the cabin. Linda stayed with him." Joe made a motion toward Roman, then handed the officer the weapon, handle first.

"Is this either of yours?"

Joe shook his head. "Roman left it behind in the remote cabin yesterday."

Linda stepped forward and handed the officer the other gun, one that was smaller and easier to conceal. The question of how they ended up with two handguns not registered to either of them should be obvious, but she wanted to make sure both were tied to Roman. "This is the gun Roman shot into the cabin. It might be tied to Dylan's death as I had possession of the M1911 after we found their hiding place last night. I wanted to hand it to you at the Primley place, but with all the chaos up there, I forgot. Good thing too. Roman didn't care who he killed to protect himself."

Officer Faruk's posture relaxed. "Can you give a statement to Offer Gates when she arrives?"

They both nodded, and Officer Faruk went back to focusing on Roman.

When Joe and Linda stepped a few feet away for

some privacy, Joe's posture sank. "She's not inside," Joe said, breathless with worry.

Linda pointed to the forest where Roman had come from. "There's only one set of footprints leading to the cabin."

"Roman's."

"Right, but there are no footprints going into the forest from the cabin. He arrived from somewhere out there. Follow the footprints, and we may find Aster."

"It's worth a try." He walked with her around Roman and the people working on him.

They said nothing as they followed the footprints back through the trees, beyond the reach of the police floodlights. Snow slowed their pace, but Linda had confidence. Roman had turned his head when she hinted that she saw Aster. She had to be in this direction. Linda felt it in her soul. Maintaining her balance wasn't easy with Zero pulling her on one arm and trying to keep her bad shoulder as immobile as one could while trekking through snowbanks. Joe limped behind. He shouldn't be walking on the ankle at all, but until Aster was safe with him, he wouldn't listen to reason, and Linda wouldn't ask it of him. Besides, she couldn't demand he take it easy when she was refusing to rest her shoulder.

"Thank you for your help. I don't know what I would have done without you," he said, his voice weary.

"I'm glad I was able to do something. I care about you and Aster."

His steps slowed. They'd been walking far enough that the chatter and noise at the cabin had disappeared.

"Remember when I told you I felt that Aster was in trouble?"

"Sure I remember. You stopped me last night as I walked Zero. Powerful stuff, those deep feelings."

"I have another feeling now."

"Really?" She didn't want to fill in the blanks. Her motivation was finding Aster, and everything pointed her in this direction, but she didn't know what condition she'd find Aster in.

"She's okay. I just know it." He picked up his pace again. "And I think you're right. It makes sense that she's out here. He would leave her back while he went to Shiver Cabin to find whatever he was looking for."

Linda was glad he had faith in her hypothesis, but the temperature wasn't looking promising for finding Aster sitting comfortably in the forest. The cold would kill quickly if she was exposed to the elements without adequate protection. Linda brought her analysis of the worst-case scenarios back under control and scanned the area for anything. Then she saw it: a shiny bit of fiberglass through the trees, the same color as the snowmobile. She picked up her pace; Zero, reading her energy, rushed forward.

They pushed through the pine branches and found Aster, her hands tied to the handles. Her head was down as though she was asleep.

"Aster…" Joe called out.

Linda checked her vitals: working but slow. When Linda shook her enough to wake her, Aster's eyes opened, but the lethargy didn't bode well for her.

"We need to get her back to the ambulance at Shiver Cabin. Can you start this?"

Joe nodded, pausing to look at his daughter. He paused. "Aster, honey, can you hear me?"

She stared at him, but any words she tried to speak came out scrambled and slurred. Her skin was pale. Joe offered her his coat. He did so without hesitation, wrapping it over her shoulders. He hesitated to open the hood, his attention on his daughter.

"Focus. She'll be okay, but she'll be better the quicker we can get her warmed up." Linda untied the cords wrapped around her wrists. She sat with her, hugging her tight to generate some body heat to get her temperature up. Aster rested her head on Linda's shoulder. At that point, she was invested in this kid's future, no matter what happened between her and Joe. If Aster needed anything in the future, Linda would do her best to assist her.

Within a few minutes, the snowmobile roared to life.

"That was faster than last time." She slid back into the seat, holding Aster in front of her. She'd be warmer and more protected if she sat between her and her father.

"I hope this is the last time." He sat and revved the engine.

There was no room for Zero this time. Linda unclipped the leash. They would need to make some time. "Sorry, boy. You need to keep up, and then you can have a deserved break."

The snowmobile cruised back over their path from the cabin with ease, making their trek out to Aster's location seem like a different odyssey. Linda checked back on Zero. He wasn't staying with the snowmobile, but she trusted his ability to follow the trail if they went too fast.

Within five minutes, they were back at the cabin. The ambulances were still there. Joe drove right up to one of them. He hopped off and got the attention of a medic. He gave them the space to do their job. They wrapped Aster in rewarming blankets and increased the heat inside the compartment.

A few minutes later, Aster slowly opened her eyes. "Dad?"

"I'm right here." He nearly wept at seeing her awake and alive. "How do you feel?"

"Better now. It was so cold out there—but I always believed you'd rescue me. You did before too."

There was so much guilt in letting Roman take her again after she'd already been pulled to safety, but he let that go. "Linda was the leader."

"That's not what she said to me at the other cabin. She said you fought off a bear."

"I might have scared him away." He was proud of that moment but happier that Linda had bragged about it for him. She was one of his biggest cheerleaders.

"Wow. I'm impressed."

He kissed her forehead. "I'm more impressed with you."

Aster inherited the best parts of her mother: her kindness, her laugh and her generosity. She was also a warrior. Strong, smart and a complete individual, not defined by her parents.

Aster turned toward him. He could see the tears

on her face. "I should never have gone with Payton. I caused so many problems. I'm so sorry."

Joe shook his head. "The only thing you did wrong last night was not telling me you were accompanying her. I can't blame you, though. I've been on your back for months, not trusting you when you've never given me a reason not to trust you."

"Really?"

"Really. I couldn't ask for a better daughter. You're more impressive than I ever was."

A bit of color was returning to her face and even a bit of a smile. "I'm better than the perfect Joseph Webster?"

"Maybe not better—but really, really close."

She nudged him with her elbow, and a full smile appeared in place of the sullen look she'd worn over the past few months. Her face held lingering images of her as a toddler and a young girl, but she was on the verge of adulthood and held herself with such confidence. She made amazing grades and had never been caught doing anything untoward, yet she was right: he assumed the worst, all the time. Faith. It shouldn't be a challenge to have faith in his daughter's decisions. It should be expected.

Chapter Twenty-Four

$\sim$

As Joe stood near Aster, who was in the back of an ambulance, Linda waited for Zero to catch up to them at the cabin. A few minutes after they arrived, Zero trudged into sight, his head and tail low. His pace picked up at the sight of her. He wiggled against her. Zero deserved an award for all he'd been through by coming out of retirement. So did Linda.

Joe shielded Aster from seeing Roman's body on the ground until she closed her eyes and rested her head back. Roman had caused so much pain: kidnapping Aster and Payton, murdering Dylan, almost killing Linda and Zero. So why didn't Joe feel triumphant over his demise?

"How are you doing?" Linda came along the side of him.

She placed her hand on his shoulder and remained silent. Thirty seconds of physical comfort without praise or judgment. The feeling wrapped him up and gave him a voice.

"I thought I'd feel relief in Roman's death, but I don't.

I didn't want him hurting anyone else, but taking his life… It's something I can take no pride in."

"I'm glad to hear it. I think we're all better off trying to help others and not harm them, even when they hurt us. But he didn't leave you much choice. I would have done the same."

"Have you ever killed anyone?"

She looked toward the coroner at Roman's side. "My job placed me in some unforgiving situations. The best I can do now is try my hardest to make the world better for everyone and see my therapist regularly."

He nodded. He understood. He wished he didn't.

Linda glanced around the area. "I'm still convinced he was looking for drugs or money. They have to be there, or why would George risk his life to go to the cabin?"

"Maybe he lost them, like he said."

She shook her head. "How do you lose thousands of dollars of drugs? I mean it's possible, but…"

One person would have the answers Linda needed: George. He was in the second ambulance, his arm wrapped. Officer Gates stood next to the open door, speaking to the medic. It would have been easy to disregard his alleged crimes based on his looks. He was a high school student on the baseball team and the son of one of the teachers, but Linda rarely went by appearances. It was too easy to see a criminal in someone without material possessions who had been through more hardship, rather than in someone with designer clothes and a college scholarship in hand.

She waved to Officer Gates, who let her approach.

"Long day?" she asked the officer.

"Too long. You?"

"Never-ending. Can I ask your passenger a quick question?"

She looked over at Linda's father. "He won't like it."

"Tell him I blackmailed you."

She laughed. "Be quick."

"Thanks."

The window in the back rolled down, and Linda leaned in. "Where did you last see the drugs, George?" She couldn't let them stay in Birch Glen, and she wasn't naive enough to think drugs wouldn't flow into town from other sources, but if she could stop some, it was better than nothing.

"I'm not saying anything without an attorney."

She waved to Officer Gates, ready to walk away. But before the window closed, she leaned in once more. "I respect your decision. I really do. As for me, I wouldn't want anyone else finding them. One overdose that's traced back to you, and you could be prosecuted for murder."

His expression tightened, then paled. "I can't find them. They sent me the wrong package—way more than I wanted. That's why Roman and Jeff were so mad at me. I would have given it back, but the package is gone."

"I happen to know someone who can find them." She glanced down at Zero.

"It was over the mantel. I swear I left it there. Why would I go against Roman?"

Linda had a mile high of sympathy for him. He was barely seventeen years old. Yet she also saw the effects of bringing drugs into a community. The lives it ripped apart, the families it destroyed. "Let's see if we can locate them and get them into a safer spot."

He didn't respond, which was fine. She shut her eyes and said a quick prayer that he'd come out all right in the end. She wanted justice to be served but also a whole lot of rehabilitation for him.

Officer Gates nodded to her. She'd been close enough to hear the conversation. Linda didn't want it to be her word against George's when the prosecutor was making their case.

Now she had another person to meet with. She strode over to her father, who stood with one of his detectives. "Could I speak to you for a minute?"

"Sure." He waved off the detective and stepped to the side to speak to her alone. "Are you feeling okay?"

"I will be. But I need access to the cabin."

He frowned. "It's a crime scene. George was shot in there."

"I know that." She'd never asked her father for a favor before, but now she was asking to help him solve this case.

"You seem to think you're still an MP. You're a civilian."

"I understand, but there could be a deadly amount of fentanyl in the cabin. Unless you have any narcotics-detection dogs in the vicinity, Zero is your best hope to finding it before it harms anyone else."

"How do you know it's in there?"

"I don't. In fact, there's a good chance it isn't in there. According to George, he put it there. Later, it was missing. Jeff could have stolen it, or George may be lying and hid it for his own gain."

Her father looked toward the cabin, then back at the ambulance, which was pulling away toward the hospital. "I don't think so. From George's reaction to Roman, he would have given him whatever he wanted. He doesn't seem strong enough to stage a coup over one of the most powerful drug cartels in New England."

"I hope you're right."

"Honestly, your instincts have been more on than mine tonight." He looked back at the cabin. "One pass."

"That's all I'll need." Carrying her father's go-ahead with her, she headed to get the harness out of Joe's Jeep. Zero saw her pick it up and jumped against her legs, tail wagging. Once she had him in the harness, she started toward the entrance. The harness told him it was time to work. Officer Faruk followed her. She preferred having a witness to her searches; two sets of eyes were always better than one, especially if one was a law enforcement officer. He could handle any evidence they located and secure the place as a crime scene.

The cabin had to be more than seventy-five years old. There was a large, open living area; a loft; and a small kitchen. The main room had a lot of wooden furniture that had seen better days and hardwood floors in need of a good sanding and polish. Since George had told them he'd hidden the drugs in the mantel, that was where she was going to start.

They walked into the main room. The fireplace was the focal point. The redbrick mantel, crowned with faded white wood, filled half the wall. Linda took a deep breath. If something were in this cabin, Roman thought it was worth killing for.

Zero sat next to her. Despite running through the snow to keep up with them on the snowmobile, he pulled at the leash, wanting to work.

"Okay, boy. Where's Mickey?" She loosened her hold on his leash and let him investigate the room.

He sniffed under a bench and one of the corners of the room and near a small table, pausing at the mantel. His focus was on the right side.

"Where would you hide drugs in a mantel?" she asked.

"Some of these older fireplace mantels have compartments in the wood." Officer Faruk began to tap on various areas of the wood. He'd slipped on latex gloves before entering the house. "Can Zero pinpoint an area?"

Linda sent Zero back, and he immediately favored the right side again, but this time, he put two paws on the wall and tried to get to the top of the mantel.

Officer Faruk tapped on the places Zero indicated, and, as if magic, a panel popped out. He looked inside. "Nothing in here, but I'm impressed anyway. I would never have found this without Zero's nose." He stepped back from the fireplace. "Now what?"

"He should search the rest of the place." She commanded him to begin again, and he covered the entire main area. They then moved to the loft. There wasn't much in there, so it didn't take as long. Zero didn't indicate on anything.

Linda had one pass. She moved with Zero and Officer Faruk to the kitchen. "Can you open the cabinet door under the sink since you have the gloves on?" she asked.

"Sure." He pulled the drawer open and allowed Zero to examine the drawer.

Zero angled his whole head inside the drawer but didn't indicate on it by sitting.

Officer Faruk shifted through the things in the drawer. "This place needs a good cleaning. I'm going to speak with the park ranger."

Linda nodded, but she was concerned that they might be at a dead end. "If George was honest about keeping the drugs here, then Zero could be picking up a residual scent but not enough to alert on it."

Zero moved on and looked inside the refrigerator and behind the oven, then finished at the back door, looking at Linda as though asking for her permission to move to another room. She led him to the bathroom. Nothing was there.

Linda left the cabin, frustrated. She had wanted to find the package and get it off the street. Perhaps George was right and someone had stolen it. Zero wasn't leashed, and Linda called him over. Instead, he romped through the snow with a puppy-like burst of energy, as he often did after a task. Except he stopped when he arrived at Trudy's RAV4. Then he sat.

Linda looked over at her father for permission to go inside. He told her to wait as he conferred with Officer Faruk. She wished she could be more a part of the investigation in an official capacity, but she understood her father's need to follow proper procedures. Officer

Faruk waved her over to the car and opened all four doors. She settled Zero down to refocus him, then sent him on to the task.

Zero circled around the car, sniffing in each door. He showed an enormous amount of interest all over the interior of the car, rushing from one door another. He hopped into the back of the SUV. There was a folded red polar-fleece blanket with a few empty grocery bags. Everything was neat and orderly.

Linda waited for him to turn back to the door. Instead, he scratched on the back of the seat. He focused more on the area beneath the seat back.

And then he sat again, his rear end resting on some of the empty bags, his attention toward the seat back.

"Could you check behind the second-row seat?" Linda asked Officer Faruk.

He nodded and squeezed next to Zero and lowered the seat back flat.

Officer Faruk checked between the folded-down seat and the back area, where Zero sat patiently. "Wow. He really is good at this." He pulled out three sandwich bags stuffed full of pills. "This is enough to pay for someone's college education."

Linda nodded and rewarded Zero with lots of rubs and some snacks she had in her pocket from earlier. He wagged his tail, acting the part of hero. After a few minutes, she tamped down her pride in Zero and the excitement in the find. Instead of continuing to celebrate, she concentrated on the person Roman had targeted through the window: George. Had he hidden this in the car and lied about it being in the cabin, or had someone else moved it into their car? The only people with access were his sister, Aster or Trudy.

Chapter Twenty-Five

Linda left Zero at her house happily licking some peanut butter ice cream to head to the police station alone. Joe had accompanied Aster to the hospital to make sure she was okay after two nights in the cold. Joe needed father-daughter time with Aster, and Linda wanted to respect their relationship without interjecting herself in the middle of it. Her relationship with Joe had no label yet. She wasn't sure what label she wanted, but she knew it had to include some connection to both Joe and Aster.

She arrived at the police station in time to hear Trudy arguing with Officer Faruk.

"You can't prove George had anything to do with this. He has his whole life ahead of him. Aster was in my car. It could have been her. Or Linda Jameson. She searched the car and could have planted it." She pointed directly at Linda.

Officer Faruk shook his head at her accusation and remained calm. "That's not possible. I was with Linda during the search."

"I don't know who to trust." Trudy's stressed appearance had grown cloudy since they'd last seen her. Her son was in the hospital with an arrest warrant waiting for him, and her daughter had been kidnapped by her son's drug supplier. Not exactly a Hallmark-movie Christmas.

"Once Forensics obtains the fingerprints on the bags, we'll have a better idea of who was involved," Officer Faruk added.

"'Fingerprints'?" Trudy turned pale.

He lifted his hands. "I wore gloves and didn't allow Linda to touch anything. The fingerprints can clear up who last held the bags."

Trudy seemed to have lost all her energy. "I'd like to speak to a lawyer."

"Absolutely."

Trudy's fight disappeared as the repercussions of her own part in this finally hit her. If she was trying to protect her son by hiding the drugs, her plan had backfired. She had almost killed both her children.

Linda nodded to Officer Faruk to thank him for keeping her out of Trudy's line of fire. She meandered back to her father's office, a simply decorated space with a few commendations and several pictures of her and her mother on his desk. His door was open, but she knocked anyway.

He looked up from his laptop. "Linda, come in."

She entered and shut the door behind her. "I just came in to check on things."

His features appeared older in the fluorescent light. "It's been quite the circus these past few days."

"I can imagine. Wish I could help."

He laughed. "You've done more than enough. I can't tell you how impressed I was by your actions last night and today without condoning your inappropriate meddling. But you made the whole case safer and easier to solve. Sending the kids from the party to the police station allowed us to get statements immediately from each of them. We tried to send several officers up to the Primley place last night, but the roads were impassable, as the snow picked up, except for the most equipped vehicles. I should never have allowed Dylan up there alone."

"He would have wanted to rush there to help in the search for Aster."

He nodded. "That's true. We called for assistance, but a full-scale search couldn't be implemented, as the storm was too dangerous." He paused for a moment. "I'd always thought a son would follow me into law enforcement, not a daughter. Somehow, I believed you would follow your mother into a quieter space, like teaching. You deserve far more credit than I ever gave to you. The fire company commended you on your handling of the situation up there. You found a safe way to move kids away from an active-shooter scene. You followed Roman and Jeff into the woods and rescued Aster and Payton, all while keeping safe in a storm and keeping Joe safe as well. You certainly are impressive, and I'm sorry for telling you that I had anything less than the utmost confidence in you."

She thought of the years he'd questioned her abilities, the little comments about her size and her ability to manage drunken marines on base. He'd always said that he was joking, but he wasn't. There was a truth to those words.

"Dad, it's easy to say that now, but your throwaway remarks about my needing help to pass through boot camp and being assigned as an MP because they needed a few women in the unit insulted me. 'Just kidding' is not an excuse when those comments drip over me incessantly. My size doesn't matter as much as my intelligence and common sense. While officers taller than six feet and above two hundred pounds do settle people down easier than an officer with my height and weight, I've been able to subdue men much bigger than me. I have to use more than my physical presence. I need a solid understanding of psychology and mental illness to do my job effectively. That requires more skill."

He nodded. "Can an old man admit he was wrong? Whatever I can do to help your footing in the civilian world, I will do."

"I appreciate it."

They fell silent. The hurt lingered, but Linda was ready to move on and allow her relationship with her father to build from the love and care he'd shown her. She had seen a change in him over the years with the addition of two female police officers and several women at the fire company. She reached out to him and held his hand.

He looked at her with something like admiration. "It's not easy watching you risk your life like that, but your mother complained to me about my job too."

"It's a heredity disease," she said with a smile. The

difference was he was employed, and she was both healing and finding a new true north. If only she could go back to work. "Just as I was ready to return to some sort of job, I'm forced to take more time to heal."

"You'll heal soon enough. Wait until you're my age. The mind is willing, but the body refuses to get off the chair."

She met up with Joe the next morning at the inn. A bit of hesitation accompanied her. Would the magic of their connection disappear now that the danger had been averted?

He sat in his office with crutches leaning next to his desk, his leg propped up on a chair next to him. A stack of papers sat next to his laptop and a large cup of coffee.

"How is Aster?" she asked.

His response came after a pause. "Physically, she's fine. Her ears and the tip of her nose turned white from all the exposure to the cold, but the doctor assured us that she'd feel better as the skin healed. Emotionally? I don't know."

"She has a good support system with you and her friends."

"And you."

"Me?"

"She looks up to you."

"How your ankle?" she asked, unsure of what to say about Aster.

He hadn't really thought about it, rushing around and making sure Aster was back at home and looking for Zero, but now that everything seemed right in the world, his focus returned to his ankle and a whole mountain of pain. "I can walk on it, but the doctor told me I need to rest a few days. Keep my foot elevated and use the crutches to keep weight off of it. Besides my own ailments, Aster needs me. I don't know how I'll be able to rest, watch Aster, and manage the inn on the busiest days of the year."

"Is there any way that someone can take your place for a day or two?"

Although no one ran the inn to the level of perfection he strived for—including himself—he considered himself skilled in finding quality people to handle the details. There were a million small pieces that had to flow perfectly for the guests to end up with an experience they would rave about. Although he saw how all the pieces came together, everyone else managed their pieces beautifully. Andy handled the kitchen with the expertise of a fine French restauranteur; Claire managed the front desk with the utmost competence; and Rebecca had full control of the housekeeping staff. Right now, Aster needed him far more than the inn did.

"Maybe it'll be okay without me at the helm," he admitted. He could try to be in his office for a few hours a day in case people had questions. They could come in and talk to him. He trusted everyone to handle things. "Yeah. I think it could work."

"I understand. I thought the whole world would fall apart if I wasn't at my post. After the accident, I was replaced with a younger MP and a goofy golden retriever named Fritz. Thinking about it drove me crazy, but after a few weeks, I realized that my value isn't my job. My value is in being my best self—so here I am, trying to be better than I was yesterday."

Joe thought about what she said. The Red Pepper Inn gave him a home, a purpose and a family that he no longer had. He had the best staff in the country. He'd grown up with some of them; others had traveled from far-off places to move to Birch Glen in order to work with him. They had his back, and he knew it. Perhaps the military had been that for Linda.

"I can't picture myself doing anything else. The inn is as much a part of me as Birch Glen."

"Did Ivy share your dream?" Linda asked.

"She wanted a home and a family. She loved the inn but wasn't nearly as invested in it as I was. I guess I always assumed everyone in my life shared my goals and aspirations. They never did. Neither you nor Ivy. I failed her in so many ways."

"How did you fail her? She had a home, a family and a handsome husband who adored her. What made her the most happy?"

He thought back to the early days of their marriage. "She was a whiz in the kitchen. She baked Aster's birthday cakes and made fresh bread twice a week." His voice faded at the end. "But I had to make one last-minute dinner request." He couldn't break the guilt.

"Were there weather warnings that day?" Linda asked.

"I never looked. It was a mid-spring freeze. The temperature dropped enough to ice the roadways."

"You couldn't have known, and neither could she. She loved you enough to want to do something special for you. Don't destroy that love with guilt and blame. It was no one's fault. Let Aster celebrate her mother without adding a dark cloud over her life or yours." Her words weren't harsh, but the reality gave him a different perspective. Maybe carrying Ivy's love inside would benefit Aster more than carrying Ivy's death.

Chapter Twenty-Six

On Christmas Eve, Joe sat in the lobby of the Red Pepper Inn and watched the magic of his amazing staff interacting with a full house of guests. Dressed in a Christmas-themed Fair Isle sweater, he sipped on eggnog and joined in a group singing Christmas carols in the lobby. Most of the guests would be hitting the slopes early the next morning. With the heavy snow accumulation from the blizzard, they would have a wonderful day on the mountain. He wouldn't be joining them. His ankle was firmly wrapped, and he had specific orders from Dr. Halden to remain off it for several weeks.

Andy, dressed in his culinary whites—hat included—walked over and slapped him on the back. "Congratulations."

"For what?"

"Mark Alexander, the reviewer for *Yankee* magazine can't stop raving about the decor, the service and especially the cuisine. Although you should be congratulating me for that part."

"You spoke to him?" A review would secure their place as a top tourist destination for the next few years. He tried not to get his hopes up, but from the look on Andy's face, it had to be true.

"Tory overheard him describing the Red Pepper to someone on the phone and saying this was one of his top stays all year. He was impressed how we handled the blizzard and said something about our exceptional service." Andy lost his composure and let out a whoop, sending a fist into the air.

Joe clapped his hands. "I can't believe it."

Andy gathered himself back together and sat next to him. "I can. We earned this."

"We did. Imagine if you never found your way back here from Jamaica. This inn wouldn't be the same without you or your mad skills." Since the renovation, the inn had earned a reputation for comfort and elegance, but Andy's cooking had taken everything up a notch.

"You had a dream and made it happen. I'm the lucky one to hop on for the ride."

"What if we cemented your presence here? I'd like you to be my business partner."

"What happened to keeping it in the family?"

Joe had once expressed his wish for his daughter to someday take over running the inn, but her dreams didn't involve guest rooms and dinner menus. As for Andy, Joe couldn't believe after so many years of watching each other's backs that Andy would question his place in Joe's life. "Number one—you *are* family. Number two—Aster's heading to Colorado this fall. I can't see a physicist happily employed at the inn."

"She's going? Are you okay being alone?"

"I'm not alone." He nodded toward the vision in red velvet walking through the door. Linda. "I have all of you to annoy me as much as a family would. And who knows, I might have a new life opening up to me."

Andy looked in the direction Joe was staring. "She's staying in Birch Glen?"

"Here's hoping."

"Here's hoping." Andy fist bumped him and headed back to the kitchen.

Joe's first instinct was to stand up and greet Linda, but she'd be more annoyed at his harming his ankle than touched by his chivalrous gesture. Instead, he waved her over.

Aster arrived at the same time. Dressed in black jeans, a white button-down shirt and a festive red-and-black plaid vest, she went over to Linda and hugged her before greeting her father and sitting down, sliding over to make room for Linda.

"Did Dad tell you?" she asked Linda.

"Tell me what?" Linda looked at Joe for an answer, but he shrugged. He wanted Aster to share her news.

"I'm going to the University of Colorado Boulder!" The excitement in her voice made most, but not all of his worries disappear. He was a dad, after all. But he had faith in the future, and leaning on it allowed him to set his daughter free to spread her wings as wide as they could go.

"That's wonderful. Congratulations." Linda hugged Aster tight, and from the look of it, Aster hugged her right back. "Your father is okay with you going away?"

"She's ready for an adventure, and she promised me she'd be home for most of her vacations." This was the right decision; Joe knew it deep in his heart.

"*Most* vacations, not all," Aster replied.

Linda squeezed Aster's hand. "That seems fair."

The smile lighting up Aster's face was contagious. Joe and Linda smiled too.

"Payton's here. I have to tell her. We promised to visit each other at school, wherever we went." She jogged off, leaving Joe and Linda alone.

"Only two days ago, you insisted that Aster would never leave the state. What changed your mind?"

"Almost losing her changed things. She has her own life to live, as do I. I can't ask her to limit her future for me. That wouldn't be fair." He stopped short of saying he hoped Linda would stick around. She'd made him realize how much he missed having someone to confide in. "You also helped me make the decision. You left Birch Glen and came back an amazing person. I hope the same for Aster."

"I'm proud of you. That decision couldn't have been easy."

Aster returned with Payton. With her brother in the hospital and mother in trouble with the police, this was not Payton's best Christmas. Joe watched how they literally leaned into each other. They'd been through a traumatic time, and it made sense they'd have a deepened connection, although Joe would make sure Aster would have access to counseling as well. Someone to speak with about everything she'd experienced. Sometimes a parent wasn't the best person for a job, but he'd still be there for oversight and mentoring and love. She wasn't completely free of him.

Linda watched as Joe and his daughter connected as individuals who had their own worries, their own needs. In order to be the best parent possible, he had to let her go, and he did. The pain of letting Aster venture so far from home etched a slight frown on his face when Aster wasn't looking. Linda wanted to give him a huge hug, tell him he was being a great dad by trusting in his daughter's decision, but she had her own news that might furrow deeper frown lines into his handsome face.

After she'd arrived home, taken a nap and dressed for Christmas Eve dinner, she'd checked her emails. Like a rainbow from a storm cloud, she'd received an offer to train working dogs at the Federal Working-Dog Center. It wasn't military, but the center trained dogs to work in federal agencies like the FBI and Secret Service. In addition, they wanted Zero to help with demonstrations, which would maintain his skills. But the center was located outside of Washington, DC, which would take her away from Joe too soon.

Joe lifted his cup of eggnog. "Care for some Christmas cheer? I can have Tori get some for you."

"No, thank you. I'm all set." She pointed to a glass of sparkling water on the table.

"What's wrong?"

"Nothing."

He took a sip and placed the cup on the table. "I want

to thank you for giving me the courage to say yes to Aster's decision."

"She'll do wonderful. Anyone who desires to travel across the country to learn from the best professors in optical physics probably is mature enough to succeed beyond even her own imagination."

"I agree. I'm excited for her."

Joe appeared wistful, with a side of pride. Perhaps she could share her own news with him. Or would it be too much to handle? Or maybe he wouldn't care at all, which would be the worst thing to happen. She didn't wish to ruin his night by trying to contain her own confusing emotions. She shut her eyes for a second, praying for clarity in her decision, took a breath and looked at him. "I have some news as well."

"Really?" His smile stumbled a bit but made a comeback a second later. "The marines want you back?"

She shook her head. She didn't want to go back to military life, despite missing many aspects of it. It was time she controlled her own destiny. "I've been offered a position in Washington, DC."

"Doing what?" That steady expression remained, not giving her a sense of his true feelings on whether he wanted her to stay.

"I'd be training dogs and their handlers, mostly in narcotics detection but other things too."

"That sounds like an amazing opportunity."

"It is." Linda had no idea what would give her the most happiness. She wanted to remain near Joe; her love had never faded for him, even after all these years. On the other hand, she needed a job, and this position would keep her in the field and allow Zero to stay active and able to be redeployed somewhere.

"There's nothing even close to that in Birch Glen."

"But you're here." She shut her eyes and breathed in the scent of a Christmas tree and the fire in the hearth. "What if I leave and regret it?"

He clasped her hands. "I wasn't supportive the last time you decided to leave, but I intend to make it up to you this time. I want you to go and see what this job is all about. You'd regret missing this opportunity. I have faith that it will work out as it's supposed to."

"I do want to see what it's all about." But she'd miss him too.

"Then go. DC isn't California. We'll have plenty of opportunities to visit."

"I guess." A traitorous tear fell down her cheek. She wiped it away and looked at the ground.

He lifted her chin so they were nose to nose. "The world is full of amazing, funny, bright and beautiful women."

She nodded. "True."

"But there's only one Linda Jameson. She's amazing, funny, bright and beautiful, too, but she's also got something none of those millions of other women have."

"What's that?" She wiped another tear from her cheek.

"My heart." He leaned in and kissed her, taking her breath and her worries away.

Snowy mountains fenced in Birch Glen, a place inaccessible by major highways. The only means into town consisted of curving roads with dips and scenery that beckoned you to stop for just a moment to absorb the calm. Joe stood on the balcony of his suite, leaning on his crutches, and paused to glance at the festive lights and the darkening sky. The town hadn't trapped Joe; it merely blinded him to other views. Strangers arrived offering new ideas for making things better, but they often missed the strength of the river flowing through town, a force that created a clear window to rainbow trout one minute and could pull a covered bridge off its foundation the next. Life here wasn't perfect; evil crept inside the borders as surely as it could in a city square. But love held this town together—and trust and caring.

He stared at the road leading away from Birch Glen. A ray of sunlight sparkled over the snow. Birch Glen was home, but with Linda leaving, it was losing its heart. Linda couldn't and shouldn't give up the chance to follow her dreams. This opportunity was too perfect to pass up. He was proud of her.

She came out on the balcony. "Did we lose you to stargazing?"

"They're shining extra bright tonight." He wrapped an arm around her as her head rested on his shoulder. He couldn't imagine letting her go again, but as his fears crashed over him, a shooting star streaked across the sky.

"Make a wish," she said.

The stars sparkled with such optimism, he couldn't help but have faith in the future. "I don't need to. Right now, for this exact moment in time, I have everything I need."

He kissed her. A kiss that was at once a connection, a belonging and a goodbye. Instead of what could have been a forever, he accepted that this kiss was merely for now. It didn't matter. He had the woman he loved in his arms and wouldn't for one minute regret any second with her.

Chapter Twenty-Seven

Christmas morning
One year later

A gondola brought Linda, Joe and Aster to the top of Stratton Mountain before the sun rose on the horizon. The temperature was a not-so-balmy twenty-five degrees, but a stillness in the air kept the chill to a minimum.

Linda and Joe carried their skis with them. Aster would snowboard down the hill with her friends.

As the sun tinged the sky in brilliant orange, a minister gave a beautiful mountaintop service announcing the birth of Jesus and telling everyone to appreciate those in their lives—the ones who were no longer with us, the ones who stood with us today and those who had yet to come into our lives.

Joe had his arm around Aster. "I'm so glad to have you back home for the next few weeks."

"I missed being here—but not enough to quit my classes in the Rocky Mountains." She seemed more mature after living apart from him since September. She was growing more into an adult with each passing day.

"I have to admit, I'm a bit jealous of your upcoming school trip to Vail. If everything works out here, I plan on joining you for some skiing on your spring break." He was confident in the staff and in Andy to leave the inn for a vacation. Having Andy invest in the business had given him some roots in Birch Glen and taken some pressure off Joe.

"I don't know if you'll be able to handle the black diamonds at Vail. They're for real experts." She elbowed him and laughed.

"I send you out for a few months, and you're already talking down your home?"

"Never. I love it here. Who knows, I might come back east for graduate school. I hear there are a few decent universities in New England. Payton's pushing me to move back someday." Aster and Payton had forged an unbreakable bond over the past year, especially after her brother was sentenced on drug charges. Her mother wasn't charged, but she made a deal with the district attorney to start a substance abuse program at the high school. Their selfishness had placed Payton in danger.

Joe smiled. "I would love you back in New England, even if you ended up in Boston."

Her expression softened. "I would too."

One of her friends called out to her, and she grabbed her board. "See you at the bottom."

He waved. "Wait for us at the lodge. I need to get back to the inn to help with the Christmas brunch."

"They can handle it without you, Dad. You need to trust them, as you trust me."

He laughed. "I do trust them. I just like being around all the activity at the inn—like I enjoy hanging out with you."

"You need a life, Dad." She sat on the ground and strapped her feet into the binding. "Catch you later." She winked at Linda and pushed off to meet up with her friends. There was laughter and smiles among the group. Joe's heart leaped. This was all he'd ever wanted for her: happiness and connection.

"I love seeing Aster so happy. Will you be okay when she heads back to Boulder?" Linda asked.

He nodded. "If you love someone, you need to allow them to spread their wings. They might come back eventually. Like you."

"You let me spread my wings?"

He bit back a smile. "I didn't complain this time when you wanted to."

"I appreciated that." She wrapped an arm around him. "It was such a wonderful opportunity to help train some of the smartest and bravest dogs in the country, but the guy in my life wanted me more."

"Me?"

"Zero. He was jealous of the time I put in with the other dogs. He wanted a career too. How could I deny him the ability to do what he was trained to do when I was offered a position with the Vermont State Police?"

"You are too good to Zero." He pulled her in closer and kissed her until another gondola arrived, welcoming more people onto the peak.

"First one down gets a back rub." She clicked her boots into her skis.

He took a deep breath and placed a hand on her arm to slow her escape. "Before you race off, I have a question I need to ask you?"

"You can ask me anything."

"What about, 'Will you marry me?'" He pulled a ring box out of his pocket and opened it. A ruby solitaire in a gold Celtic knot glistened in the morning sun.

"Are you sure you want to get married again?" Her smile fell, and she became so serious, he almost regretted asking her in such a public spot.

He held her hand. "I've never been more sure of anything. The last few Christmases before you came back into my life weren't anything to celebrate, so I thought we could break the cycle with something that would make me and your parents happy. Aster's pretty excited too."

"Everyone knows but me?"

He'd asked Aster when she arrived home, and she had been more than thrilled to have Linda become part of her life on a more permanent basis. Linda's parents seemed relieved that she'd finally be settling down, although Joe knew more than anyone that marrying him would never slow her down for the things she wanted to do. "They all know the question, but only you know the answer."

"Hmm. As of right now, only I know the answer. Leaves me in a position of power." The devious smile on her face reminded him of why he loved her so much.

He had no idea what she'd say, but the sparkle in her eyes hinted at a positive outcome.

"I guess I could wait until we get to the bottom of the hill." He turned toward the skis he'd placed on the ground, trying not to give away his excitement.

"The answer is yes," she called out so loudly, it echoed across the mountain. Skiers waiting at the top of the mountain clapped for the newly engaged couple.

Joe turned around so quickly, he nearly fell to the ground. She wrapped her arms around him and kissed him, her love warming every part of him.

After sliding the ring onto her finger, he put the box in his pocket and clicked into his own skis while Linda stared at the ring. He loved her too much to give her even the slightest bit of an advantage, so he pushed off before she could get her gloves on. "A back rub sounds good about now."

He raced off but wouldn't have to wait long for Linda to catch up. She was a strong skier. Not that it mattered, because he'd already won the most important prize: her heart.

He'd had so little faith when she'd returned into his life, but her love for him and his for her were enough to conquer mountains.

* * * * *

Get 3 FREE REWARDS!

We'll send you 2 FREE Books plus a FREE Mystery Gift.

FREE Value Over **$20**

Both the **Love Inspired®** and **Love Inspired® Suspense** series feature compelling novels filled with inspirational romance, faith, forgiveness and hope.

YES! Please send me 2 FREE novels from the Love Inspired or Love Inspired Suspense series and my FREE gift (gift is worth about $10 retail). After receiving them, if I don't wish to receive any more books, I can return the shipping statement marked "cancel." If I don't cancel, I will receive 6 brand-new Love Inspired Larger-Print books or Love Inspired Suspense Larger-Print books every month and be billed just $6.49 each in the U.S. or $6.74 each in Canada. That is a savings of at least 16% off the cover price. It's quite a bargain! Shipping and handling is just 50¢ per book in the U.S. and $1.25 per book in Canada.* I understand that accepting the 2 free books and gift places me under no obligation to buy anything. I can always return a shipment and cancel at any time by calling the number below. The free books and gift are mine to keep no matter what I decide.

Choose one: ☐ **Love Inspired Larger-Print**
(122/322 BPA GRPA)

☐ **Love Inspired Suspense Larger-Print**
(107/307 BPA GRPA)

☐ **Or Try Both!**
(122/322 & 107/307 BPA GRRP)

Name (please print)

Address _____ Apt. #

City _____ State/Province _____ Zip/Postal Code

Email: Please check this box ☐ if you would like to receive newsletters and promotional emails from Harlequin Enterprises ULC and its affiliates. You can unsubscribe anytime.

Mail to the **Harlequin Reader Service:**
IN U.S.A.: P.O. Box 1341, Buffalo, NY 14240-8531
IN CANADA: P.O. Box 603, Fort Erie, Ontario L2A 5X3

Want to try 2 free books from another series! Call 1-800-873-8635 or visit www.ReaderService.com.

---

*Terms and prices subject to change without notice. Prices do not include sales taxes, which will be charged (if applicable) based on your state or country of residence. Canadian residents will be charged applicable taxes. Offer not valid in Quebec. This offer is limited to one order per household. Books received may not be as shown. Not valid for current subscribers to the Love Inspired or Love Inspired Suspense series. All orders subject to approval. Credit or debit balances in a customer's account(s) may be offset by any other outstanding balance owed by or to the customer. Please allow 4 to 6 weeks for delivery. Offer available while quantities last.

Your Privacy—Your information is being collected by Harlequin Enterprises ULC, operating as Harlequin Reader Service. For a complete summary of the information we collect, how we use this information and to whom it is disclosed, please visit our privacy notice located at corporate.harlequin.com/privacy-notice. From time to time we may also exchange your personal information with reputable third parties. If you wish to opt out of this sharing of your personal information, please visit readerservice.com/consumerschoice or call 1-800-873-8635. **Notice to California Residents**—Under California law, you have specific rights to control and access your data. For more information on these rights and how to exercise them, visit corporate.harlequin.com/california-privacy.

LIRLIS23

Get 3 FREE REWARDS!

We'll send you 2 FREE Books **plus** a FREE Mystery Gift.

FREE Value Over **$20**

Both the **Harlequin® Special Edition** and **Harlequin® Heartwarming™** series feature compelling novels filled with stories of love and strength where the bonds of friendship, family and community unite.

Get 3 FREE REWARDS!

We'll send you 2 FREE Books plus a FREE Mystery Gift.

FREE
Value Over
$20

Both the **Mystery Library** and **Essential Suspense** series feature compelling novels filled with gripping mysteries, edge-of-your-seat thrillers and heart-stopping romantic suspense stories.

HARLEQUIN
PLUS

Try the best multimedia subscription service for romance readers like you!

Read, Watch and Play.

Experience the easiest way to get the romance content you crave.

Start your **FREE TRIAL** at
www.harlequinplus.com/freetrial.